An investigation

into

DEATH ON BEN NEVIS

in October, 1983

by

Sidney Harber-Bridge

N.D., LL.M., B.A., Dip. H M.

The Seider Press, La Groudiere

Writing as Professor Harry Calvert, Dr. Harber-Bridge has written many other books, mostly inconsequential and all of them boring. You don't want to know.

ISBN: 978-0-244-04420-6

To Coco, whose bed I have had the privilege of sharing for many years

Climbing vocabulary

Belay – tying onto rock for security

Chock – metal or other block to assist in belaying

Karabiner – metal loop to assist in belaying

Lead/leader – first person on rope

Sac – container for gear etc., carried on back

Seconder – second person on rope

Shit – expression used when falling off

Shit! – expression used on landing

Sling – rope or canvas loop to assist in belaying

FOREWORD

This is an account of a hitherto unexplained death on Ben Nevis, the highest mountain in the British Isles, in the late autumn of 1983.

Death in the mountains is almost always dramatic and often tragic in the classical sense of the term. It is much more rare for tragedy and mystery to coincide as they did in the case considered here.

That the tragedy was revealed and the mystery unravelled was largely due to the efforts of Detective Inspector Ann ("Annie") Chisholm who was, I believe, one of the first women to be appointed to such a post in Scotland. This is largely her account of events described as told to me although in a few minor respects, I have been able to supplement it from other sources. A few gaps in the account have necessitated the use off a little imagination on my part.

Mountains and mountaineering form the backcloth of the drama which unfolded. Despite this, the story which emerged was not, essentially, a mountaineering story of interest only to those obsessive freaks whose chief preoccupation seems to be risking their necks clambering up rocks. It is, rather, a story of ordinary common-or-garden human weakness. Greed plays a large part in it, lust a lesser one. There is even a spark of courage here and there.

The scene of the drama was the great north face of Ben Nevis. A national poll amongst mountaineers would result in it being voted the greatest cliff in Britain and even accomplished alpinists hold it in high regard. The best way to describe it is to ask the reader to picture in his mind's eye a great dome reaching nearly four and a half thousand feet above sea-level and then to imagine a gigantic clawed hand clamped down on top of it and tearing the entire northern half away. What results is a great irregular cliff, averaging some 2,000 feet in height, buttressed by a series of great ridges which are separated by steep, scree-filled gullies.

From east to west (left to right as you look at the face from the north) the cliff measures more than a mile and is topped by the summit plateau. The actual summit of Ben Nevis is towards the eastern end of this plateau. The high point of the western end claims title as a separate summit, Carn Dearg, from which fall the great walls and buttresses which have witnessed some of the great advances in modern climbing.

The events with which this account is concerned took place on the eastern part of this cliff, here supported by a series of ridges and buttresses which were the scene of the early, classic, developments in Scottish climbing and which tends still to be preferred by old-timers such as Dr. Alan Jeffries, my constant climbing companion, and I. The most striking feature here, indeed on the whole face, is Tower Ridge.

Tower Ridge itself is a great ramp thrown down the centre of the face from the summit plateau, its toe reaching right to the lowest part of the face. It is as though the Almighty had decided that the great cliff was altogether too much and built up this ramp as a stairway to the top of the mountain. For climbers, it is an obvious and striking line to follow and is rightly considered as Britain's greatest mountaineering route. For many climbers, including some of those with which this narrative is concerned, it is the Mecca.

Time was, up to half a century ago, when Tower Ridge

was regarded as a testing challenge, even for accomplished mountaineers and it is still a fairly demanding proposition in serious winter conditions. In summer, however, it is now regarded as little more than a scramble. It is chastening, as one puffs one's way proudly up it, to encounter young hard men, in training, jogging down it. Only at one point does it pose a climbing problem and even that has more of a psychological than of a physical character. This is the notorious Tower Gap, beyond which lies the easy summit tower and the top. Here, just before the Gap, the ridge is at its narrowest – almost knife-edged. Alan strides along it; I crouch and crawl. At the gap itself, it is as though some ancient gigantic warrior had smashed his sword down on this very sharp edge and cut a cleft in it some twelve feet deep and no more than about six feet wide. The adventurous, indeed, leap it. Lesser mortals can easily lower themselves from one edge, down onto a large block to which the rope can be attached. Then, lowering further, off the block, it becomes easy to lean across, resting on one's hands against the far wall. Having reached this position, it is no problem to step across onto good holds and then up on "jug-handles" onto the far, summit, side of the Gap. Nothing to it, technically, that is.

The problems are purely psychological. It probably helps to be blind or at least short-sighted, for there is no easy way off this ridge. Its sides are extremely steep and at the Gap the flanks fall away almost vertically for hundreds of feet into the flanking gullies, Tower Gully one side, Glover's Chimney, leading into Number Two Gully on the other side. When you get to the point where you have to lean across, it is almost impossible to avoid imagining where the leaning would lead to if you were ever so slightly off-balance.

It was hereabouts that the main events with which this account is concerned unfolded.

It would have been much better if Annie had recounted the events herself but she is, as would be expected, a very busy woman. So the task has fallen to me for no particularly compelling reason. As will be seen, my connection with the affair was slight, though crucial. Alan had a rather larger part to play. In the course of the investigation, however, I met most of the leading characters involved in it. And of those of us who were in some way involved, I alone am presumed to have nothing better to do. Some eight months ago, I received an offer from my employer which I would have been mad to refuse and took early retirement. The others all claim, as busy people still "on the make" in their respective careers do, to have more important things with which to occupy themselves.

As far as I am concerned, the main reason for taking on the job was because Annie asked me to. She seemed to think that twenty two years editing an academic journal somehow qualified me for it. We all agreed that the events with which it deals should be recorded and she said it would "keep me out of mischief!"

I have written it with her blessing. She has read the manuscript and approves of it as a whole although there are one or two particular respects in which she would be inclined to express some doubts.

CHAPTER 1

Alan and I have been climbing together, on and off, for many decades. We first roped up together when we were students in Edinburgh in the early fifties. We used to get a lot more done then than now. Alan is a consultant psychotherapist at St. Beatrice's hospital in Perth and manages to get all too little time off for my or, for that matter, his liking. We have climbed practically everywhere in Britain where there are the easy moderate long mountaineering routes which are to our liking and we usually manage to spend a couple of weeks together in the Alps in summer. If only he would retire, we could manage a lot more but he is dedicated to his job at what he embarrassingly describes as his "funny farm" and there seems little immediate likelihood of his giving it up.

As things are, when we get the chance to combine business and pleasure, as occasionally happens, we usually seize it. The cause of research into hypnotherapy might have been more speedily advanced if conference organisers had chosen venues other than Munich and Grenoble thus facing us with the irresistible temptation to skip the odd session or two in favour of nearby attractions. One of the infrequent opportunities that we manage to contrive came about when I was asked to acts as external examiner of a doctoral candidate In Dundee.

That particular activity was scheduled for the Monday. On the Friday evening, I had driven to Birmingham and had managed to get a sleeper to Edinburgh. I ought to have had plenty of time to wake up, wash, shave, dress and have tea and biscuits and stroll to platform 1 at Waverly station for the

Dundee train. In the event, a combination of bridge repairs *en route*, putting us twenty minutes behind schedule and a steward who forgot or neglected to wake me found me frantically pulling on my gear, grabbing the sac and "sprinting" for the connection which I only just managed to make. Then, to put the most charitable interpretation on it, Alan and I "missed" one another at the station in Dundee. He insists he was there waiting for me but I would hardly have missed him if that had been so and I still maintain that the idle sod was in bed. As it was, I set off to walk and lost another half an hour. The delicious great greasy fry-up assembled for us by Alan's gorgeous wife, Clare, occupied us for an extremely well-spent hour but although it did much to restore morale, it was still well after ten before we found ourselves roaring across Scotland in Alan's ancient Jaguar on the way to Fort William. I mention all this only to explain my irritability but for which we would probably not have ended up where we did that day.

We were headed for Ben Nevis, which overlooks Fort William. We usually go there when neither of us has a positive and overpowering urge to try elsewhere and that is often the case. Tower Ridge was one of the possibilities we had in mind that day as we sped (and Alan does not hang about) towards Spean Bridge just a few miles northeast of Fort William. Alan fancied the Ridge, I suspect because taking one look at me, knackered and unshaven, he thought it would be quite enough; although it was May, winter conditions prevail longer on the Ben than anywhere else in Britain and it is not unusual for snow and ice to survive the summer in some of the dark recesses of the gullies. On the Ridge, ice would probably choke the "eastern traverse", the niche via which one negotiates the

Great Tower just before the Gap. I rather resented this implied slur on my competence and fitness and fancied something a bit more prestigious – something I could bash peoples' ears with when the climbing club met at the Duke of Wellington. On the Ridge we were quite likely to find tough winter conditions on what would nevertheless be regarded as an easy summer doddle.

These were the truths lurking behind the words as we argued the toss over a cup of coffee at Spean Bridge. I prevailed. Alan agreed and we decided to climb in the area to the west of the Ridge, below and around Number Two Gully. Exactly what we were going to do would wait until we saw how things were on the mountain. We would have a choice of easy ways or a combination of somewhat harder things, which I preferred. Alan kept his counsel, as he does. When we are together we still maintain the pretence that we are getting better and better and I always argue for something that is really a bit too much for us. Alan recognizes that we are past it and functions as a sobering and restraining influence.

I won the battle to avoid picking up the tab for coffee and we headed off for the golf club car park and thence for the Allt a'Mhuillin, the valley which leads up to the foot of the face where stands the Charles Inglis Climbing hut.

As we plodded across the golf course and then headed off up through the mud and scrub, the profile of the lower parts of the ridges kept coming tantalisingly into view as the low cloud thinned and then thickened again. As I mounted steadily at my "Guide's pace" (so-called in reference to the slow regular pace which Alpine guides use but in my case determined by an inability to go any faster) Alan forged ahead, as he always does. By the time I arrived at the Hut he had been there for some minutes and had unpacked butties lovingly assembled by Clare and poured a couple of cups of coffee. He obviously needed the break. I was all for pressing on; it was already late in the day and the weather was most unpromising but I had not gone all that way for nothing.

"What do you think?" he asked, meaning, *"You're not so bloody lunatic as to want to go on in conditions like this, are you?"*

"Well we might as well press on up for a while and see how it goes," I replied, meaning *"I'm buggered if I've come all this way just to eat a butty at the bottom and go back down."*

Five minutes later, we were crossing the stream and mounting the scree below the western flanks of the Douglas Boulder, the 700-foot high crag which forms the foot of Tower Ridge.

The cloud had now thickened and seemed to have settled in for the day. Visibility was down to less than one hundred yards. The forecast had not been good; conditions were ideal for the sanctimonious type of mountain rescuer who seems to delight in being able to say, after the event, "They shouldn't have been there at all on a day like that." It was I who insisted that we go on. It was not stupidity; it was worse. We had only two days and this was one of them. I was not going to waste it sitting at the bottom twiddling my thumbs.

We managed to find the foot of the subsidiary gully by which we intended to climb the lower part of the face. There was still a sufficient build-up of snow in it and we climbed it easily except for a couple of steep bits near the start which Alan led. In a little more than an hour we had emerged onto easier ground which seemed to fall away to our right, although visibility was by this time so poor that we couldn't be sure. You could literally hardly see the hand of the man in front of you. Nevertheless, we thought we knew where we were and were confident of finding the Number Two Gully area where we would have a choice of ways of getting to the summit plateau. The easiest way was no doubt via Number Two Gully itself but I was still hankering after something a bit more memorable and vaguely remembered reading about a way to the right of the gully, up the Comb, the buttress which flanked it on that side.

When we encountered rock, we assumed it to be the Comb. At this point, Alan momentarily triumphed and insisted that we go up the snow to the left, intending to climb out via what we took to be Number Two Gully. As the ramp of snow began to narrow and steepen, doubts began to crystallise. I, however, had faith and when a steep and icy cleft opened up on the right, I was sure I had found the way up the Comb which I hankered after. I tried to persuade Alan but he wanted nothing to do with it, saying it looked too hard for the likes of us (by which he meant me). It promised, nevertheless, the "something memorable" that I was after and, as much to put an end to the argument and confident that I would soon give it best, Alan eventually agreed to let me have a go at it.

To be honest, it didn't really appear very promising initially. It started up a near vertical wall, which seemed improbable but I thought I remembered (wrongly as it turned out) that the hard part of the route that I had in mind was at the start, so I pressed on. After about fifteen feet of grunting and scrabbling about, at the end of which I had almost changed my mind, I managed to tie on around a spike of rock and was able to hang on for a couple of minutes of physical and emotional restoration. Even so, looking up, I was still on the point of giving it best when I noticed, peering through the mist, something red. It must, I thought, be a rope sling or something like that. Anyway, it established in my mind that we were on a recognized route. Somebody had been there before us.

He was still there; and that's how it all started.

As I heaved my way upwards, it soon became obvious that it was not a rope sling. It looked more like a bit of a cagoule or anorak. Then there was what appeared to be a stocking and a few seconds later, it was clear that it was a stocking, a stocking, furthermore, complete with contents.

It takes a little time to believe the evidence of one's senses in a situation such as that. I can recall vividly seeing, very clearly without being able to credit it. "That looks like a leg," I said to myself, "but since it can't be a leg, what is it?"

Alan tells me that he then heard me mutter "Jesus Christ! Jesus Christ!" in a manner and tone quite unfamiliar to him.

"What the hell's the matter?" he yelled up.

"There's a body, jammed in the chimney here," I said.

CHAPTER 2

Annie Chisholm is a remarkable woman. You have to be a remarkable woman to be a detective-inspector in the Fort William CID and at the same time, deputy leader of the Spean Bridge mountain rescue team AND a woman; and that is by no means the whole story. I had always rather assumed, in my prejudiced way, that all policewomen must be hard-nosed bitches or butch and, anyway, at least half-fascist to have gone in for a job like that in the first place. Annie Chisholm, whom I got to know very well, soon disabused me of all such notions.

She is one of those people whose basic seriousness of purpose and diligence, not to say old-fashioned goodness, is disguised by a veneer of genuine frivolity and love of life – one of the work-hard-play-hard types. People who really care, as Annie does, about other people and what the world does to them have to cope with life in one of two ways. They pray; or they laugh. Otherwise they have nervous breakdowns (or, as Alan once put it 'drop their bundles and come to live at the farm'.) Annie copes by good humour.

She is 33 years old and already has eleven years' police service behind her. She entered the force with a double handicap, being a woman and a graduate. Joining the police force was, she says (and I believe her) the first important positive decision she made in her life. Until that point, it was just a matter of following the normal course along which young people are carried. She did well in her Highers at her school in Gatehouse of Fleet in Galloway, moving on to read French and Hispanic Studies at St. Andrews. Diligence yielded her the opportunity to spend a fourth year there reading for honours and her seriousness of purpose in the endeavour gained her a very good upper second. With a touch of the good luck, which is essential in all such cases, it could have been a first and her later life might have been totally different. Even as it was, but for a streak of perversity (which I suspect is indispensable in a really good detective) she would probably have continued in the direction in which her upbringing and experience thus far had pointed her and gone in for teaching.

At that point in her career, however, she rebelled against the blandishments of her parents, themselves both teachers, rejected the advice of tutors and turned her back on the academy. She undoubtedly believed, as she still asserts, that she was not clever enough but in that she does herself an injustice. As it was, she flirted first with the idea of joining the WRNS. She might well have gone ahead with that, were it not for her brother's counsel which suggested that there was "More to it than a life on the ocean wave and sharing a hammock with the naval equivalent of Steve McQueen." Probation work then tempted her briefly. She was for a while quite serious about it but a couple of days tramping the sordid round with a probation officer scotched that idea. Its was, therefore, distinctly odd that she should have finally opted for police work which, to the uninitiated, looks very much like sweeping up the detritus of humanity, but in uniform.

She traded this information with me one boozy evening at the Craddach Hotel. About the only time I really feel like a pint of beer is when I first come down off the hill and then I want it straightaway or the urge leaves me. Almost invariably, outside Scotland, I contrive perversely to get down before the pubs open. When I become dictator, the licencing laws will become the first thing to go because the urge rapidly dissipates and I am denied a rare pleasure. In spite of the fact that I don't really like beer at any other time I persist in drinking it on an evening out in the mountains. I had just ordered one for myself and was about to drink it when she came in.

Even when she was in uniform she looked quite dishy. I say "even in uniform" but perhaps I should say "especially in uniform" – since I have graduated to dirty-old-man status I have rather gone for the black-stockinged authoritarian thing. But out of uniform, she immediately had me striving to look twenty years younger. The gut was hastily drawn in, the back straightened and I strove to reach a couple of inches taller than my five foot eight.

That couple of inches mattered since she was almost my height. That was not all we had in common. She had ash-blond hair and it must have been about the time that mine started to turn white. Her front, too, sported a protuberance though it was a foot or so higher up and distinctly more attractive than mine. She was not exactly stunningly dressed; she sported a white polo-necked sweater with its arms pushed up to her elbows and a pair of corduroy breeches. Not very sexy, you might think. Breeches often give the impression that the hips are round the knees but not in Annie's case. Her face and forearms were that rich honey colour that you get from the hills in winter rather than the ephemeral dark tan you bring back from a week in the Med. Her teeth were probably not quite as white as they seemed as she recognized me and came smilingly towards me but they appeared to me to me to be, like the rest of her, perfectly formed. It was all rather confusing – she could probably have done for everyone in the bar in unarmed combat and had been climbing some of the hardest routes around since her days with the St. Andrews Climbing Club.

I was hopelessly charming as I greeted her and asked her what she would like to drink trying to recall, as I did so, how long it was since I had trimmed the hairs in my ears. I had a quick bet with myself before she replied – if not butch, she at least had to be a tomboy and probably prided herself on downing as many pints in an evening as the rest of the lads. I lost. She asked for a "Stock" explaining, when it was clear that I had never heard of it, that it was a sort of Italian brandy and I wished that I too had gone for something rough and fiery.

* * *

That was the second occasion on which I met her. I have to say that although I remember practically every other detail about our first meeting she made singularly little impression on me. To be fair, it may be because the circumstances were not such as to encourage erotic interest to burgeon.

I came to no harm when I fell off in Glover's Chimney that day. The sling I had managed to fix on the rock spike held me short of the deck though not short of Alan who had bravely thrust a shoulder against the rock beneath me to break my fall. He owed it to me; I once stopped him with a shoulder on Tryfan when he came shuttering down a groove. I had felt I should; unable to find anything else I had belayed round a tuft of grass, though it was a large tuft.

Flattening him in Glover's Chimney improved neither his confusion nor his temper. "What the fuck is going on?" he

10

demanded as he pulled himself to his feet.

"There's a body jammed in that cleft up there," I gestured, gasping; "Up there, about 25 feet above the spike. Look – see, there, up there, on the left. Can't you see it, the red thing, there? It's an anorak or something. It's a body."

It's not the sort of thing that happens to you every day and Alan accepted it only reluctantly. "What the bloody hell are you talking about?" It was all too much. He had not wanted to be there; he had not wanted this weather. He had not wanted me to descend on him from a dizzy height and certainly not because I had come across something so complicating as a body.

"Are you certain?" he eventually asked. "It could easily look like a body but be something else."

"Look" I tried calmly to reassure him. "There's no doubt about it; there's a leg, there's a body." Then, doubting, I added "unless it's a very convincing dummy," which, recalling the activities of film-crews working on the Ben, we admitted to each other was a possibility. Still "I know it's crazy, but there it is. You can see the leg clearly and you can make out an arm, a hand. The rest of it is encased in the ice. Really, it is, but if you want to go up and make sure, I'll hold you."

"Stuff that for a lark" was his intended and expected reply to that invitation. "Look; are you sure?"

"For Christ's sake, Alan, I've told you – I'm sure. What do you expect me to say? 'Oh sorry, no, I'm mistaken, it's not a body; it's a sodding telephone kiosk!"

"Ok, Ok, let's get organized," he soothed. And we did get organized, or rather, he did. We honestly didn't know exactly where we were and couldn't be sure of finding the place again, so he had the wit to fasten an orange plastic survival bag using a couple of slings to fix it to the rock and off we went down.

We had no difficulty finding our way down. Unless you're bent on finding difficulties you just follow the line of least resistance off this part of the mountain and you arrive back at the stream in due course. A further hour found us back at the car park. We decided it would make more sense to head off straight to the police station rather than messing about with the 'phone. In any case, mature reflection tended to dispel any sense of urgency, which had irrationally surrounded the events of the past two hours. It was of no great moment whether our newfound friend up on the Ben descended today or tomorrow.

We soon found the station and within minutes were recounting the details of our macabre find to the duty desk sergeant.

"You're sure it was a body are you sir; you're quite sure he was dead, are you? We've had no reports of anybody going missing lately."

"Look, sergeant," Alan summoned up the tattered remnants of his patience, "I know it sounds improbable and it is possible that it's a dummy dumped there by some filming outfit, but Dr. Sanderson," nodding in my direction, "knows what he saw and there's no doubt whatever that there's something that needs looking into. Please, we're hardly the types to hoax you about a thing like this. There IS a body, jammed in a chimney somewhere up there in the region of Number Two Gully. It's not urgent – the poor sod is comprehensively dead, no doubt about that. But there is a body, or something very like one, up there."

"Very well, sir. If you'll just take a seat for a couple of minutes, I'll see if the Inspector is available."

We sat for a couple of minutes, then for another couple. Why did it need an "Inspector?" We could say all we had to say to anybody. Why were we waiting? We'd said everything already. It dawned on us that we were ravenous. We'd had a fairly strenuous not to say stressful day and had kept going on a couple of butties and a cup of coffee. Alan went back to explain our situation to the desk sergeant and we headed off to the restaurant just up the main street. "The Inspector" would pop up the road as soon as possible and have a chat with us.

Fort William is still some way from enjoying a world-wide reputation as a gastronomic centre but things have improved enormously over the past few years and within ten minutes our eating irons were poised over steaming plates of home-made steak and kidney pie and Brussels sprouts miraculously saved from over-cooking and glazed carrots. They had even dug up a half-decent bottle of Clos Vougeot, grossly under-priced, and the "beating-your-head-against-a-brick-wall-lovely-when-it-stops" rationale of the mountain experience seemed irrefutable.

From time to time we had glanced towards the door over our Taliskers. I did so now, again, preparing to launch my attack on the pie and, as if on cue, a police person of the female variety appeared and looked around, presumably for us. I immediately assumed, in my sexist way, that this must be the Inspector's skivvy with a message and signalled to her just as her gaze settled on us. She probably didn't need the signal. She would have a description. It would have been nice if that description had been couched in terms of athleticism and charm but Scottish police economy had probably settled for "two elderly gentlemen" and, if so, it had clearly been adequate.

I must confess that I was taken aback when she joined us and introduced herself as not merely "Inspector" Chisholm but as "Detective Inspector" Chisholm.

"DETECTIVE Inspector?"

I queried, striving to camouflage my sexist preconceptions behind a diversion. "Do you think that this is the sort of business that calls for your talents, then?"

She laughed with an air of unseriousness disarming in a policewoman. "No, certainly not as a detective but I'm on the Spean Bridge Rescue so it will short-circuit things if I take it on". That surprised us as well. Would there ever be an anti-climax to this day? Still, we were all agreed on one thing. It was hardly a job for the CID.

We could not have been more wrong.

CHAPTER 3

Annie Chisholm reckoned she had a pretty good idea who it was before they even set out to recover the body.

That turned out to be a difficult and gruesome task. By the time she got the details from the two elderly gentlemen it was too late to turn out. They would hardly be up to the foot of the face before nightfall and, even if they were, visibility was still much too poor for them to spot the orange bivvy bag which marked the site. It was as well they waited, anyway, for the next day dawned bright and clear, if cold, and they were able to spot the bag, even without binoculars. This brought forth the comment "What the hell were you doing up there?" before they reached the Hut a good 1,500 feet below it.

We had set out with Annie and two of the Spean Bridge team just in case we could be of any use in finding the site again but we were not needed. We were able, however, to watch progress from below. Another detachment of the Spean Bridge Rescue had set off up the Ben the easy way from Fort William. From what we had said, it might well turn out that the easiest way to recover the body, if that was what it turned out to be, might be to winch a man down from above to recover and then lower the body. That was to be the second party's task. That, in the event, is what they did.

It was, I must say, a bit humiliating to observe the ease with which the young "crag rat" who accompanied Annie's lot swarmed up the cleft which had caused me so much difficulty the previous day. He soon got to the body and, we later learned, confirmed our worst fears. He tied himself on above it and took a considerable time to cut it clear of the ice with his axe.

Meanwhile, the team above got the winch into position above the chimney and lowered one of their number on the rope which he maneuvered, not without some difficulty, to the site of the corpse. The two of them manhandled it into a black plastic body bag. That can have been neither easy nor pleasant although exactly how unpleasant we were only to learn later. They then tied themselves and the sac into the rope from above and were duly lowered.

The poor sod was obviously long and indisputably dead. It could have been left to gravity to bring him most of the way down; he would not have minded. There is, however, a strange compulsion to treat the victim of a mountain death with a tender respect. Even a couple of old sawbones who would think nothing of butchering away all day in a path lab would have behaved likewise.

The preliminary report from the pathologist, Dr. Kenny, turned out to be singularly unhelpful. We had already heard the nauseating detail from the lads who got the body down. It lacked a head, and, indeed, still lacks a head for it has never been found and presumably still lurks up there on the Ben. Dr. Kenny was able to confirm that death had been due to decapitation: all the signs were that the head had been wrenched off in a fall. Even had it not been so, the other injuries were so grave and numerous that death would have almost certainly have been instantaneous. I was not aware, until this incident, that the human frame could disintegrate quite so readily in a fall but it is apparently by no means unknown. One member of Annie's team had actually seen the process take place. Watching a party at work on one of the extreme new routes on the Droites in the Mont Blanc range, his gaze had been distracted upwards to settle on a solo climber prescribing a series of gentle arcs down the wall and then breaking into two on a protruding rock before it continued its apparently slow but now complex descent to the glacier below.

Other information about the victim needed the specialist skills of the pathologist. The corpse had been on the mountain for quite some time. It might have been as much as two years, possibly even more. Storm, frost, exposure and the appetite of creatures living on the Ben had all added their bit to the normal processes and the body was in an advanced state of decay. Fingerprinting was out. It was, however, male. The age could have been anything from a raddled forties to a well-preserved sixty plus. When Annie asked, "Can you not be more precise?" Dr. Kenny, irascible as ever, had apparently asked, "what do you want me to do? Saw the bones and count the rings?" The build was described, unhelpfully, as medium and the height as "probably more than 5' 8" but less than six feet."

This vagueness did not greatly trouble Annie. It was precise enough for her. She was now fairly clear in her mind whose body it was they had brought down. Two men had gone missing in the area over the last two years. The body had almost certainly to be one of them. When people went missing, someone almost always missed them. Not absolutely always; only fifteen months or so ago, they had brought down a severely injured woman from just above the Hut and nobody had claimed her. She was last heard of recovering in a Glasgow hospital where she had not even claimed herself. This, however, was very unusual.

Of the two unaccounted for one was a young lad, Greg

17

Douglas, from Glasgow, only in his late teens. Already he had established a reputation on some of Scotland's most demanding climbs. He had set off on his own, apparently to the Cairngorms, but young men such as he are free spirits and if whim had directed him to the classic hard routes of Ben Nevis, it is to those that he would have gone.

It was not difficult to speculate what would have happened. He would have tried something that bit too hard, that bit too soon, pressing himself that vital edge beyond his limits. His final resting place might never be known. His age, however, suggested that it was unlikely to be the cleft in Glover's Chimney.

The other one was Sandy Piper, a telephone engineer from Berwick whose circumstances had strongly suggested suicide, although none would object if some other verdict were eventually returned. Aged 57, he had been made redundant from a job he had held for nearly thirty years the year before he disappeared. He had, however, picked himself up from that and got himself another job only to be made redundant again four months later on the last-in-first-out principle. He then disappeared. Those who knew him had said that the second redundancy had finished him. He just couldn't pick himself up again. Had he had a wife or family that might have carried him through it but he hadn't. There was talk of a "dark lady" across the border for Sandy used to disappear practically every weekend. It was, however, much more likely that on these mysterious occasions, he travelled north rather than south for he was an avid collector of "Munroes" – Scottish summits of more than 3,000 feet.

Some who purport to love the mountains have death

wish about them. Others are less extreme but nevertheless take the view that since it must happen, let it be in the hills.

A friend of mine retired, went off walking in North Wales, did the Snowdon horseshoe on a superb March day when it was at tis best, then sat down on the summit of Lliwedd and died of a heart-attack. He must have been a happy man. Sandy Piper was, it appears, of this type and the speculation that he had simply decided to end it all after the second redundancy in November 1982 seemed solidly based since he had not been seen since.

Except that it wasn't he.

Annie had been slow to arrive at this conclusion but there was no escaping it, unless, that is, Sandy Piper had been living rough in the mountains for eleven months through the extreme winter of two years ago and then popped into Fort William to buy a new anorak to die in.

It was as a result of going through the routine that this surprising fact had surfaced. It is routine in such cases to compile an inventory of gear, clothing, possessions etc. found on or with the body. In the instant case, it had been a very short inventory. What remained of the corpse had been clad in ordinary underwear, shirt, an old pair of worsted trousers and a Guernsey sweater. One foot had lacked a boot but that was not unusual; boots were usually the first things to be wrenched off in a fall. One odd feature was that it wore a harness but there was no rope although that could easily have resulted from tying on carelessly or making a mistake in roping solo. He must have been on his own or surely a climbing partner would have reported the fall and called out the rescue.

There ought to have been a sac but, if so, it was still

either hidden somewhere down the mountain or, more likely, appropriated as manna from heaven by some ill-equipped Glasgow lad up for a few days. There was, however, the anorak. It caught Annie's eye because it was a very expensive new jacket of a type she herself had her eye on, made up out of one of the new magic materials which resist the rain but let the sweat out. So expensive and new was it that although Annie had read about it in the gear columns of the climbing mags and resolved there and then to buy one it had not yet worked its way up to the top of her list of expenditure priorities. She was surprised, when she checked, to discover that it had been available for as long as seventeen months. She was able to be even more precise about the particular item in question because one of the pockets contained, in addition to a plastic whistle and one of those Scandinavian compasses, a sales tag from "Cragsman's" in Fort William.

Johnny Irvine, who ran "Cragsman's" had got hold of half a dozen of the anoraks as soon as they became available. He had spotted them as a likely profitable line at the Harrogate Show and he had been right. He was able to identify the one which had done service as a shroud as belonging to this initial half-dozen and was able to narrow it down a bit more than that.

"Aye," he revealed to Annie, "I sold them all, fairly quickly. I can't be certain when the last of them went but I think it was before the end of the year, the year before last that is." Most of them had gone by the end of the summer. When he came to check his records, he corrected himself. Four had been sold in the same week in October.

"Would you be able to say who you sold them to?"

asked Annie.

"Sorry, no. At least, not if they paid by cash or cheque." He pondered for a moment but then continued. "But I might be able to help if they were paid for by credit card. They're good spenders – too good for their own peace of mind some of them. The credit card slips have names and addresses. I use them as a mailing list; do quite a lot of business that way."

For the next five days, Annie Chisholm blessed her luck. On the tenth of October 1983, one Edward Jenkinson of Burnhope Crescent, Consett, Co. Durham used his Barclaycard to purchase "Goods" to the value of £109.95 at "Cragsman's" in Fort William. It was possible that he had bought 22.71 water bottles or approximately six and a quarter pairs of Saunders rock boots. It was, however, more likely that he had purchased a McKinley jacket for £109.95 for that was its exact price.

CHAPTER 4

DI Jack Birtley was only superficially liberal. "Their business, isn't it? If the three of them want to wander off and shack up together, nothin' to do wi' us, is it? It's not illegal – consentin' adults and all that" but you were left with the distinct impression that if he could have made it illegal, very illegal, he would have done so like a shot.

Annie had hoped that a 'phone call or at most two would have settled the matter. Then it appeared that three or four might be necessary. Now the Consett force were being unbudgingly unenthusiastic about the whole business and a Gordian-knot cutting visit seemed to be the only option.

The Super was extremely reluctant. "Look, Annie, what have you got? Yet another bloke coming to grief on the Ben. It looks a million quid to a bent ha'penny that it's this bloke Jenkinson and you've got all the evidence about that you're going to get at this end. Leave it to Consett. Their pigeon now. They'll be only too willing for you to do their work for them but you work for me, remember? Anyway, you shouldn't be on the case at all. Any reason to suppose it's a CID job?"

Annie shook her head.

"No, I thought not. You get back to your own work."

"But Super," pleaded Annie, not without the hesitation appropriate to a female graduate. "There's nothing on at the moment that Dick (her sergeant) can't handle, at least for a couple of days. The break-in at Bundy's was almost certainly Alex Marsh so that's just a matter of waiting for him to turn up and we've reached a dead end on the rustling."

The conversation continued in this vein for a few more

exchanges before they did a deal. If Annie would tack her Saturday onto his Friday, she could go, said the Super and to be fair to him that was reasonable enough. Any fears Annie might have had about discrimination from that quarter were now seen to be totally unfounded. She had had a wall to climb with the Super initially but he was a reasonable man – both reasonable and a man – and no reasonable man could deny Annie's varied qualities for long. And, if she was honest with herself, it really was not a CID job. The truth was that something about it rankled and she wanted to get it sorted out for her own peace of mind.

She had started by 'phoning Birtley, her opposite number at Consett. It was obvious from his tone right at the start that he did not take kindly to the idea of a woman doing a man's job. Annie had got used to this and almost expected it from a Geordie. It was what she called the "Cultural burden"; the psychological cost of pushing a pram round the block was vastly greater in the case of the British male with the average macho upbringing than in the case of his missus. Expecting it, however, did not make it any easier. "Oh Christ," she thought, "here we go again."

Fortunately for her, Jack Birtley was the victim of opposing pulls. He certainly wanted to make his views known about a mere girl doing a man's job, but he had his professional pride and he certainly did not want anyone, especially a woman, to think he wasn't on the ball if he could possibly avoid it. Frequently enough he couldn't but the Jenkinson business had excited enough interest in the small tightly-knit community to stay at his fingertips.

Where there is scandal there is often crime and it was

this connection, larded with simple prurience which had attracted him to the Jenkinson business. When Annie had asked him if one Edward Jenkinson of Burnhope Crescent, Consett, was missing, he had been able to reply, intriguingly and accurately, "Yes and no." Yes, nobody had seen hair nor hide of him for fifteen months or so but no, nobody had reported him missing. One reason for that, certainly, was that the only person likely to report him missing was his wife, Rosemary, and she was missing too. And that was not all. Jenkinson's best friend (and Rosemary's as well, smirked Birtley to himself) Arthur Welsby, was "missing" also. They appeared to have all upped and offed together leaving poor Agnes Welsby on her own. So there was the scandal. It took rather more effort to find the crime that went with it.

What had happened was clearly not a spur of the moment thing. And the central character in it all Arthur Welsby.

Arthur Welsby had led an exemplary life. At 18, he had gone straight into Lloyds Bank from school and had served them faithfully, if not always effectively, for the next 39 years, culminating in some years' service in the Blea Moor branch just outside the town. It was, it is true, a small branch and it might be thought to indicate that Arthur's career in the bank had been mediocre rather than meteoric. If so, that was apt, for Arthur was a mediocre man.

At 22, he had married Agnes, daughter of friends of his parents. It is tempting to excuse Arthur's subsequent behaviour by reference to his immaturity when he married, except that he was one of those people who is born old. He had married Agnes, and she him, because it was the obvious thing to do. He had not loved Agnes; love, as opposed to lust (as later events established) seems to have been an alien emotion to him. It was as if the Almighty had omitted it when putting Arthur together. He was aware that procreation, just as much as marriage, was the thing to do, and at first, he tried. But he saw it as an operation rather than as an experience and after a mere five months of marriage Agnes, to whom sex of any variety of which she was aware had never appealed, had contracted the "headache" from which she had been suffering ever since. Arthur did not mind much; he had not really wanted children, nor sex, at all events not as it now presented itself to him and it was only when Rosemary, Jenkinson's wife, entered on the scene many years later that his horizons broadened. He had, from the first, been no more ambitious than he was romantic. He was early marked out by the bank as a man likely to remain pedestrian for the whole of his career. When, after twenty years' service, Arthur's failure to secure promotion had become positively embarrassing, he had been offered the assistant managership of the Blea Moor branch of the bank but had declined, saying that he "didn't want the responsibility". This state of affairs had been tolerated for a further nine years, by which time it had been made clear to him that redundancy was the only alternative to a move. He thus finally became assistant manager and, four years later, manager at Blea Moor.

Socially, the Welsbys saw few people other than family and the Jenkinsons. Gradually, nieces and nephews went their way and older relatives died off. The Welsbys did quite well out of the attrition. He was an only child and grandchild and she was one of only two. None of the family was wealthy but many had long standing as members of the property-owning democracy and the proceeds of three and a half estates of no mean order had come their way during the ten years preceding these events. They were, as a result, comfortably off. Nearly £150,000 was conservatively invested on bank deposit (on favourable terms, of course) and in building society accounts, Treasury bonds and unit trusts. As was proper, all these investments stood in the joint names of Arthur and Agnes except for one building society account in Agnes's name.

Arthur had known Edward Jenkinson since primary school days. They had gone to the same grammar school, the Welsbys paying for Arthur. Although not at first close friends, they saw quite a lot of each other once they had joined the Boy Scouts together. That was when they started to go hiking and eventually Youth Hostelling together, graduating in due course, via the local climbing club, to the higher hills. It was an odd feature of Arthur's personality that he should develop such interests until, that is, you realized that the nearest he ever came to emotion was in his dislike of company. Edward had long since ceased to remark upon the fact that Arthur said and enthused little when on the hill.

There was hardly any more to Edward than there was to Arthur. He had passed his County Minor scholarship examinations and might conceivably have made rather more of himself had the need arisen but he was earmarked from the start for a partnership in his father's estate agency business. This had duly come to pass despite a blotting of the copybook early on. His father never made any strenuous effort to train Edward in the mysterious ways of estate agency; it was something, he thought, that "rubbed off". After all, either you could sell houses or you couldn't. Edward was, however, young and healthy and the office abounded in marriageable young secretaries, one of whom was Rosemary. The only fatherly advice Edward ever received was "don't shit on your own doorstep, lad" and even this, with considerable help from Rosemary, he contrived to ignore.

Two strategies prevailed for upward mobility at Rosemary's school and no one ever figured out why some girls embraced one and the rest the other. Some strove for academic attainment. Others, including Rosemary, perhaps more realistically for those days set their sights on landing a suitable male. Romance might enter into it but some, including perhaps Rosemary, were unlikely ever to fall in love with the man. It was, it is true, a lottery. Many such marriages obviously failed ending in valium if not divorce but that seemed not to matter.

She might have become a nurse and angled for a doctor but something like a vocation seemed necessary for that and Rosemary had none. The most commonly trod path was secretarial college and business and this Rosemary had followed. Those were the days when, if you were qualified for a job you were likely to get one and Rosemary went straight from college to the firm of Jenkinson & Son, Estate Agents.

Rosemary was not a beautiful girl by any means. She was tall and well built although not fat. If you were aiming to be kind you would describe her as statuesque. If you were striving to be honest you would have to admit that she made you think of the East German swimming team or, perhaps more attractive, to some, the non-steroid-warped type of discus thrower. It was an odd feature of their eventual marriage that she, statuesque, and he, stout, were practically identical in size. Jeans and sweaters were interchangeable and she constantly irritated him by wearing his bedroom slippers. He had assumed that her knickers would not do the job for him and had never tried them but when she sought to borrow his shirts, there proved to be two good reasons why they proved inadequate for the purpose.

In one other respect, Rosemary's stature had an undesirable effect. An enthusiastic member of the local amateur dramatic society, she had an exceptional thespian talent, but her compelling physical presence meant that she was unlikely ever to be cast as a Juliet. There was, nevertheless, something about her that attracted a certain type of man, one seeking protection, perhaps. This suited her fine.

Although erotic experience had totally eluded her, she never questioned the need for symbiotic relationships with men which, her experience had taught her, our society demands. It was what one did. She was furthermore, very good-natured and perfectly capable of liking men and enjoying being liked by them. In Jenkinson's Edward was the obvious target and it was a relatively simple matter to office-politic her way to becoming his secretary.

This makes it all sound very single-minded and cold-blooded but it was not so at all. Although she would not have recognized what it meant, Rosemary was amoral and became accustomed, with little resistance on her part, to sitting behind the desk with Edward, his hand up her skirt, hers down his trousers, content that it obviously pleased him. It was almost inevitable that, sooner or later, she would become pregnant anyway, simply as a result of pleasing him more, even had it not coincided with her other ambitions. When it did happen, the rest followed. Edward did not mind at all; he saw only an infinite recession of groping and writhing and asked for little more. So they married in haste and were not greatly perturbed when Rosemary miscarried.

Some say that a rewarding sexual relationship is an adequate foundation for marriage. Perhaps, between some spouses, it is. But once Rosemary became a housewife, as married women generally did in those days, Edward acquired a new secretary and the cycle began again. Rosemary, her security threatened, successfully fought off this and later challenges but Edward's behaviour persistently eroded any emotional tie between them and their marriage became a shell – very like that of the Welsbys, really, which I suppose was one of the things they had in common. The others were Bridge, which obviated much of the undesirable necessity to chatter and the outdoors, for they all enjoyed walking and Rosemary, at least, was prepared to be led up the easier climbing routes which was all that Edward and Arthur aspired to.

Edward and Agnes were sufficiently quiescent for this to be a satisfactory compromise with life. It would have been equally so for Arthur but for his late development and even that might not have come about had it not been for Rosemary.

Rosemary always liked to enjoy herself. For a long time she was content with social status, coffee mornings, bridge evenings and the occasional walk and/or picnic with the Welsbys. But this all depended upon her having a man. In the final analysis her attractiveness for a certain type of man and the reassurance which his admiration lent her were all she had, or indeed could have according to the prevailing social norms. As she approached forty her mind, much preoccupied with insecurity about her husband, started to wonder where she had gone wrong and her psyche started to insist that all was not as it should be. But opportunities for her to steer a different course were rare. She felt she had a lot to make up for. She became aware of an opportunity however when she felt Arthur's thigh pressing against hers under the bridge table. Curious to know where this might lead, she pressed back. Arthur's interest was confirmed on a camping weekend when, given the opportunity, he indicated intentionally and unambiguously that he was, as he perceived it, anxious to function as a source of enjoyment, if that was what she wanted. Why not, she thought. What else was there? She knew Arthur was weak but that quite amused her.

No more happened for some months. The opportunity did not present itself. Then Arthur's secretary left. There is little doubt that irrelevant considerations entered into Rosemary's appointment as her successor but she was, after all, well-qualified and Arthur insisted maturely and honestly that he didn't want another of "those dolly birds" and all four thought it would be a good thing if the job went to "one of the family". Had Arthur's and Rosemary's interests coincided exactly, it might well have turned out to be a perfect arrangement and the parties might have lived happily ever after and I been spared the need to write this history. Unfortunately, they did not.

The trouble was that Rosemary was essentially an old-fashioned girl. Utterly uninhibited in her desire to secure the affection and protection of a man by pleasing him and willing to put up with the most unusual erotic contortions were they appropriate to that end the ultimate prize would wisely only be made available within the confines or, at all events, the close environs of a marriage which would confer security. In the privacy of the manager's office at Blea Moor she would, whenever asked lead Arthur to the point of shuddering uncontrollable frenzy. She underwent no crises of conscience about Arthur's kneading her breasts and she realized that you have to stop a man boiling over when aroused, so she would help him with that. But she early on drew the line, memorably informing Arthur on the first occasion when he tried to press matters to the ultimate that "the only man to do that to me must be my husband."

In his lucid intervals Arthur would never have contemplated divorce from Agnes in order to marry Rosemary. Marriage was indeed the last thing he wanted from her. The first and only thing he wanted was gratification for his newly discovered lust and he had no difficulty reconciling this with the continuation of the placid *modus vivendi* which the years with Agnes had caused to evolve. But that was during the lucid intervals. All that changed the day he gasped, pressed again to the point of no return but, reminded by Rosemary of the conditions for proceeding further, "Oh, marry me, Rosemary". "Yes, Arthur, alright!" she had said with a strange lack of enthusiasm and off had come the knickers but from that time on, the problems, as well as Arthur, mounted.

Arthur thought at first that he had won. Restored to sanity and involved in a discussion about dates and strategy that he could no longer avoid, he had pointed out, quite sensibly, that they were hardly in a position to act precipitately. If they went ahead immediately, there would be no end of difficulties. He would hardly dare show his face at Rotary and he doubted he would be retained as a lay preacher. As for his future in the Masons, well, he could forget about that. He even wondered if the bank would keep him on; customers, especially the women, might not like the idea of having to deal with an adulterer. And if he tried to move, he would be unlikely, at his age and with his record, to get another job. He could not touch a penny of the family fortunes without Agnes's concurrence and they both knew, all too well how she kept tabs on every penny. So, somewhat reluctantly, Rosemary settled for four years ahead when Arthur could retire on a full pension and they could move to Saltburn or Whitby, or even the South coast and live happily ever after. She had reservations, but by now she had firmly fixed her future on Arthur. She was happy to describe herself as "loving" him. Without this, the grotesque wrestling on the office floor might have lost some of its justification.

So far as Arthur was concerned, something would turn up during the interregnum of four years. He would manage, somehow, to negotiate a withdrawal from the situation in which he had precipitately landed himself. He had not expected what, in the event, did turn up to turn up at all, let alone so quickly. Even then, had Rosemary not been his secretary and opened his mail, he might have kept from her the offer of early retirement which arrived exactly one month after their first coupling. As it was he arrived at the bank that morning to find Rosemary flushed and excited at the news. All their problems were over. The Bank, anxious to close uneconomic branches, including Blea Moor, had offered Arthur the choice of retiring on a full pension or accepting redeployment which effectively meant demotion in all respects other than salary. The latter was not an attractive prospect and had it not been for the complication added by his affair with Rosemary, Arthur might well have decided after mature consideration, to retire. To do so now, however, would be to remove the last obstacle to the implementation of Rosemary's plans. That made it very difficult.

It was another of Arthur's many faults that his initial impulse was always to say what he thought his listener would most like to hear. It was a serious deficiency in a banker and had got him into no end of trouble in the past. He fell victim to it again now. "Marvellous; that's marvellous," he exclaimed with commendable conviction, going immediately into a clinch to get his breath back. He never did. The only intervals in a morning otherwise occupied by Rosemary's scheming chatter she filled by rousing Arthur to heights never previously attained. By lunchtime he was emotionally and physically drained, had agreed to accept early retirement eight weeks thence and then to announce the news to Agnes and go off into the sunset with Rosemary.

And so the die was cast. What remained was the crime. For some people social conformity is an all or nothing thing. Remove any one single social constraint and the whole edifice comes tumbling down.

Until Rosemary came along, Arthur had never even had a parking ticket. Admittedly, it helped to have a fellow Mason in the local traffic branch but, even so, Arthur would never have knowingly taken the risk. Now, suddenly, he was on the brink of losing his job, leaving his own wife to run off with the wife of his best friend and quitting Rotary, Chapel and Masons. He supposed that there was some sort of a life to be had, albeit uncertainly, in Saltburn or Whitby, but he was not at all sure it was the life for him.

He would have been surprised to learn that Rosemary's ambitions did not chime perfectly with what she supposed his to be. She had not communicated her preference to Arthur. Rather than Saltburn, Whitby or even Eastbourne, Rosemary had in mind the possibility of a cottage in the Highlands and perhaps, even, a small villa in the Med, funds permitting as, if things turned out well, they possibly might.

CHAPTER 5

Annie set out for Consett in her own Metro HLS before dawn on the Friday. She was unsure whether or not the use of one of the police cars was warranted and chose to err on the right side. She had treated herself to "The Flying Shed" (as Dick referred to it) when it first came out. It suited her pocket and if you put the front seat forward and the back seat down it made a satisfactory bivvy for one or even, on two memorable occasions, a crowded one for two.

Her tentative schedule was settled. She wanted, first of all, to glean whatever remained to be gleaned from Jack Birtley. He was now as keen as she was. It had dawned on him that if her speculation was correct he could close a file. Then she had to see Agnes Welsby to try to find out what she could about the seemingly odd relationship between the couples and the reasons why three of them had disappeared. Finally, the bank might be able to offer some useful information about two of its late employees and perhaps even about Edward Jenkinson.

From Jack Birtley she got little more than she already knew. The neighbours, it appeared, had a theory that the Welsbys and the Jenkinsons went in for a bit of wife swapping (why, wondered Annie, did nobody ever go in for husband-swapping?) But in Annie's experience that was a practice almost entirely confined to pornographic books or films. The only actual instance she had ever come across was when a flat-mate at St. Andrews casually mentioned that her parents engaged in it and Annie had still not decided whether or not her leg was being pulled. What she later heard confirmed her scepticism. It might conceivably be true of Edward, Arthur and

Rosemary but it definitely didn't fit Agnes. Perhaps that was the explanation – perhaps the more adventurous three had decided to strike out together and leave the more staid Agnes at home.

She was wondering how to broach this somewhat delicate topic when she rang the bell at the Welsby residence. It was a substantial mock-Tudor detached house which, in a less depressed and more salubrious area would have fetched a fair old price. Not less than sixty or seventy thousand in Fort William she reckoned. She had rung Mrs. Welsby beforehand so her presence would not come as a surprise. But even so, Agnes seemed at first reluctant to admit her. A timid face crowned by greying and poorly-permed hair peered round the half-open door. "Why the reluctance?" Annie wondered.

"Inspector Chisholm," Annie nodded smiling.

"Er, please come in; do come in," Agnes finally hesitatingly invited, opening the door more fully and stepping inside. Annie entered and was ushered into a sitting room striking in its undistinctiveness. Walls which had been painted a plain white now some years ago had turned to a muddy cream. Stained fingers and an abundance of ashtrays suggested that Agnes at least was a heavy smoker. But there was nothing on the walls – no pictures, photographs, plates or any of the standard decoration that graces the average suburban home. There was a bookcase but it contained not dog-eared paperbacks and well-fingered favourites but four neat rows of uniform volumes – one blue, one red, one green and one yellow. You could usually glean some background about its occupants from the house in which they lived and Annie wondered whether this room reflected the drabness of Agnes,

Arthur or the marriage.

"Do sit down."

Annie was steered towards a near-antique tub chair by the side of an ornate mock-log electric fire.

"As I mentioned on the 'phone, Mrs. Welsby, I wanted to ask you a few questions about Edward Jenkinson. You and your husband were close friends of the Jenkinsons, I understand."

"Well, yes, I suppose. I'm not sure I would call them 'close' friends but we used to see quite a lot of each other."

"I wonder if, for a start, you could give me a description of Edward Jenkinson," – Annie had already gathered from Jack Birtley that Edward satisfied the few criteria for identification offered by the body brought down from the Ben but it made an easy factual start to the interrogation and would lead into the news she had about how Edward had met his end.

"Yes, yes, Edward you say. Certainly. What exactly do you want to know?"

"Oh, you know, just the simple things. How old was he? How tall was he? Was he small, medium, well-built; that sort of thing."

Annie gradually established what she already knew. Edward was 57 years of age, 5'8" to 5'10" tall and of medium build. The description probably fitted half the males in Britain.

"I've been told, Mrs. Welsby, that you haven't seen Mr. Jenkinson for fifteen months or so. Is that correct?"

A minimal "Yes."

"Can you remember exactly when you saw him last?"

Agnes hesitated. "I can't remember exactly. We used to see quite a lot of them, you know. It would be about the start of October."

"October, 1983, that is?"

"Yes, that's right."

"I gather Mr. Jenkinson went away with your husband."

"Yes."

"And Mrs. Jenkinson."

"Yes," almost inaudibly.

"And you've seen none of them since."

"No, I haven't."

"Mrs. Welsby, are you sure you can't remember exactly when you last saw them? I would have thought you would remember something so ...well, memorable as that."

"No. I meant I couldn't remember when I last saw Edward. I saw my husband the day they left... I mean HE left. They must have all gone together but I didn't see the Jenkinsons that day."

"You knew, though, did you, that your husband was leaving? He must have told you, surely. You must have discussed it."

Agnes was noticeably more agitated and confused. "No, no, I didn't... I knew nothing about it."

"But you must have known something, surely. When did you find out? Didn't your husband tell you ANYTHING about their plans?"

"No, I tell you; he didn't." A lengthy silence, broken by Agnes. "It was his last day at work. We'd talked about having a holiday but nothing definite. He wasn't one to celebrate things. He came home from work, a bit earlier than usual. He didn't say anything. Just went upstairs. I wondered what he was doing; I'd made some tea. I called up to him that his tea was ready and he came down. He had his hat and coat on. He had his climbing sac over one shoulder and a large suitcase." Agnes dried up.

"What did he do then? What did he say?"

"He just left… he said 'I'm leaving you Agnes' and left." Agnes's voice became indistinct; her eyes began to glisten.

Annie came back to it from a different direction but Agnes was consistent and adamant and insisted that she had had no inkling whatever of what was about, to happen. She had not seen the Jenkinsons for some time previously; they had not talked about it. Her answers were minimal. She spoke only in terms of observed facts except that she inferred that "they must all have gone off together."

"What did you do when he left?"

"What could I do? There was nothing I could do, nobody I could turn to. I just stayed here. I tried to watch some television. I made an omelette but I couldn't eat it. Eventually I went to bed. I don't know what time it was. It was late but I couldn't get to sleep." Agnes choked: "It was the worst day of my life."

One point was slightly puzzling. Annie tidied up: "You say you had nobody to turn to, but there were the Jenkinsons weren't there? You didn't know, at that stage, did you, that they had all gone off together?"

Agnes elaborated in somewhat greater detail than Annie had expected: "No, not at that stage I didn't. Actually, I rang Edward, I rang them, but I got no reply. I assumed they were out. I rang again later – I kept ringing. I went round the next morning but there was nobody there. The car was gone so I came back. I kept trying for several days then it dawned on me that they had left too."

"So you had no idea where they were all going, what they were going to do?"

"No, none at all."

Annie confirmed that all four of them spent time in the mountains. Their favourite venue was the Highlands, more particularly Ben Nevis and, most helpfully of all, Edward and Arthur were always going on about Tower Ridge. Oddly, although Agnes answered all of Annie's questions, she had none of her own. This, in Annie's experience, was unusual. People were usually curious where the police were concerned unless, that is, they knew bloody well what it was all about. Otherwise they almost always wanted it confirmed straight away that they were not about to be lifted. When you first started it was a bit off-putting when everybody seemed to have some murky past to hide then you realised it was just the 'authority' thing; the irrational guilt made them assume they had something that they should hide even when, as was usually the case, they hadn't. But Agnes had asked no questions.

It was time, Annie thought, to let her know. "I'm sorry, Mrs. Welsby, I really ought to tell you what this is all about. I have some news, I'm afraid. Last Sunday we recovered a body from Ben Nevis. It had been there for some time, we think…"

"You needn't tell me," Agnes's face contorted "It was Arthur, wasn't it?"

Odd, thought Annie. Never mind, "No, no, Mrs. Welsby, it wasn't your husband. It appears to have been Edward Jenkinson."

"Oh, no," snarled Agnes, "It's not Edward. Edward is alive and well alright. That I do know."

40

CHAPTER 6

Agnes's bitter exclamation had rather rocked Annie back on her heels. It was the bank which detailed the explanation. If Jack Birtley had done his job properly she would have wasted less time and been spared some embarrassment.

The evidence for Edward Jenkinson's survival was simple. The Jenkinsons had had over £4,000 in ready cash in their interest-bearing current account and Edward had continued to draw on it, indeed overdraw on it for several months after his disappearance. He had, furthermore, tested his Barclaycard, cleared monthly by direct debit, to destruction. The anorak was merely the first item of evidence of an orgy of extravagance. The rest of what the bank had to say was a bit of a mare's nest but at the end of it Annie had clear evidence of most of the elements of a substantial and premeditated fraud. And it appeared to be mostly Arthur's doing.

Over the eight weeks between the hatching of the plot with Rosemary and its execution, Arthur had painstakingly realized all his and Agnes's investments. He had not stopped there. He had gone to the limits of his personal authority in raising a further advance on the house. To the proceeds of these transactions had been added the lump-sum payable on his retirement and he had assigned his pension rights to a London broker for £42,820. Twice during the eight weeks, the account had been cleared by the issue by the bank of a draft, payable to bearer, the first for £50,000, the second for £44,618. The proceeds of the assignment had been taken in large denomination notes. Arthur had had to concoct a cock-and-bull story about a customer wishing to present a draft for the proceeds of sale of a house for cash in order to explain to head office the need for such a large sum being made available at Blea Moor. Although much of this was not merely odd but improper (Arthur could well have got the sack for it) it was not, in itself, obviously criminal. What did need explaining, however, was Agnes's part in it. Almost the entire Welsby estate, such as it was, was held in joint names and Agnes must have signed a flurry of orders and transfers for Arthur to get his hands on it. Indeed, they bore her name. Could she really have been so stupid as not to realise that something was afoot?

That, at all event, was what she claimed when Annie returned to tax her with the question. Yes, Arthur had given her a lot of things to sign during the eight weeks prior to his departure but it was only when he left that it dawned on her what the true reason was. He had, she said, told her that the market was about to take a tumble and that for the time being cash was the best investment. She always left these things to Arthur; she just took his word for it. Arthur had always managed their money in the same way. At least, he had done the half-decent thing by her. He had left her her own building society account and another one as well. Life was not easy but she could manage at least for the time being.

Annie had one more thing to discuss with Agnes. It was now distinctly possible that Agnes's belief that the body was that of Arthur had some foundation. When the three of them left Consett, Arthur presumably had tucked away in his wallet the banker's drafts payable in cash to bearer without question and large denomination notes worth in all nearly £140,000. Annie now faced the possibility that she was on CID business after all. Perhaps it was not an accident; perhaps somebody, most likely Edward but just possibly Rosemary or the two of them together had done away with Arthur. Many people would find £140,000 and no questions asked very tempting. Who knows to what extent Edward and perhaps even Rosemary genuinely enthused about the idea of a romping *ménage a trois* in the sun.

She became more convinced when she asked Agnes about Arthur. He was the same age as Edward and there was no more than an inch difference in height, if that. Arthur had been quite trim in his youth but had grown quite stout later but the stoutness would have been fat rather than bone although the body had been in no state to warrant such a distinction.

"I'm sorry to press you on this, Mrs. Welsby, it must obviously be very distressing for you," (though it was not noticeably so, thought Annie) "but can you think of any distinguishing marks, anything at all that might help us identify the body?"

Arthur, it turned out, had been bald but Annie decided to spare Agnes an explanation of why that information was singularly unhelpful. Otherwise, Agnes could think of nothing – no scars, no missing fingers etc. which might be helpful although "there is one thing" ventured Agnes. "Arthur took a bit of a fall on Scafell Buttress oh, seven or eight years ago. Broke his right leg. It mended alright but they had to screw it together with a plate or something."

"And they left it in?" enquired Annie.

"Oh yes; so far as I know," was the reply.

Odd that Dr. Kenny, the pathologist hadn't mentioned it, thought Annie. A 'phone all soon established why.

"Good God, woman. Do you really think that if there'd

been something like that I wouldn't have mentioned it? It's about the most unidentifiable corpse I've ever come across. If there'd been something like that of course I would have told you. And while I'm about it, it didn't have three legs either."

Of course, it remained possible that the plate had been removed and that Agnes either knew or had forgotten about it – or was lying, Annie cautiously added for herself.

It took the whole of a lunch at the "Cross Keys" for Annie finally to accept that she had drawn a complete blank. She had gone to Consett quite chuffed with the neat bit of detective work she had done with the anorak and credit card slip believing that it was just a matter of confirming Edward Jenkinsons' identity. Unless his ghost had been drawing cheques on his account, however, it could not be he. The situation she had uncovered in Consett reeked of mystery and she could hardly believe it was unconnected. She thought she had found the connection with Arthur and had there been a plate on the skeletal right leg of the corpse that would have been absolutely conclusive. Its absence appeared to be equally conclusive the other way. It could not be Arthur.

And it certainly wasn't Rosemary! The three of them were likely lying there on some sun-soaked beach on the Costa del Crime, even if they weren't fully qualified, living it up at Agnes's expense. The body had certainly been sporting an anorak of exactly the same type that Edward Jenkinson had bought but it must be one of the others paid for by cash or cheque. That really wasn't so surprising, thought Annie. Practically every anorak bought in Fort William would end up on the Ben, many of them almost immediately. So that was that. There had only been a one in six chance it was his in the first place.

All this she explained to the Super on her return to Fort William. His reply was predictable. "I told you you were wasting your time. The sexual practices of the Sassenach must have been a very interesting diversion for you. Perhaps now we can return to the boring, mundane business of keeping the "Queen's peace in Fort William. You're back at square one, I know but you know that happens all the time. Don't fret about it. It's sad. Some poor sod came to grief but nobody's missed him; nobody seems to care. Leave it alone now and the answer will come to you. If there's ever going to be an answer, that is."

But it would not go away. One reason was the very same one that the Super had offered for leaving it alone. Nobody HAD missed him. Nobody seemed to care. You would think somebody would, wouldn't you? Admittedly, he might be any one of hundreds who had gone missing in places like Kidderminster or Huddersfield without any reason to suppose they had ended up on Ben Nevis. But such a one would not have been "transported", Startrek-wise, materializing suddenly a thousand feet below the summits of the Ben without leaving some sort of trace. Annie tried to leave it behind her on the Aonach Eagach Ridge on the Sunday but it dogged her the whole way like the spectral companions which some solo climbers in the high Himalayas had reported being conscious of on the rope behind them. She was still wondering what, consistently with the Super's exhortation to leave it alone, she could do about it when she entered the CID office on Monday morning.

"What have you got on today, Dick?" she asked of the colleague who shared the office.

"On, nothing urgent or pressing," he replied, sniffing hopefully at the scent of a pretext for taking a break from the interminable routine of the rustling business. "Why? Got something for me?"

"It's about that business on the Ben."

"Yes. I gathered from the Super that the Consett business turned out to be a false trail."

"I'm not so sure," said Annie, and she meant it. Three solid flesh and blood human beings had departed the Consett scene in rather odd circumstances and none of them had been seen since, all this at much the same time that an unidentified body had begun its long vigil on the mountain. And at least one of the three had been there, in Fort William, buying an anorak of exactly the same type as that found on the corpse. She couldn't let it go just like that. Even if the Consett imbroglio had no direct connection with the body on the Ben it came too close to let it drop entirely. It might be possible to trace the trio in Fort William. They were unlikely to have dashed into the town, bought an anorak and then dashed out again. Even if there was no direct connection, there might be an indirect one.

"How do you fancy a day 'phoning round the hotels, boarding houses, B. & B.s etc. Ask them to check on the second and third weeks of October, year before last. Find out if any guests nicked off without paying bills and whatever, especially if they left anything valuable behind – that sort of thing – anything suggesting they intended to return but didn't. And take the afternoon off. Have a walk up to the CIC Hut. There's a key at the desk. Take a look at the logbook and see who, if anybody, was up there at about that time. If there was, they might have something to tell us."

Dick's search yielded an unexpectedly rich harvest. It was surprising how many people nicked off without paying a bill, odder still how few proprietors bothered to report it. Another cost passed on to the customer, Annie supposed. The trawl later resulted in several red faces in various parts of Britain and put away one entrepreneur who, it turned out, had been living on nothing but the best in various parts of the North for several months previously but who is now savouring the fare of Peterhead Gaol. There was no trace of the Consett trio however, at least not obviously so. At first, Annie thought they, or some of them, might have surfaced in a different guise for at the end of the process of tracking down the defaulters three remained unaccounted for. Odd that it was just three who could not be traced. Once she started to find out something about these latter three, however, that possibility dimmed.

Two parties made up the three. One bloke had been put on the list as a result of Dick's trek up to the CIC Hut to look for potential witnesses. It was an unpopular time of the year and a lot of the types who used the Hut did not bother with the logbook, even assuming they could write which was a big assumption in some cases, thought Annie. Of the few who had bothered to make an entry all but one had been easily traced. They were either known to Annie or her colleagues at Spean Bridge; or a 'phone call to a local station had done the trick. In one case, however, contact had not been made. One Ken Gerrard of the Notts Mountaineering Association had inscribed his intention to "Solo Point Five, conditions permitting, otherwise train on Obs. Or Twr Ridge". "Obs", Annie assumed, meant Observatory Ridge, parallel to Tower Ridge and about 300 yards to the east. Observatory Buttress, between the two ridges, was a bit hard for "training."

The Notts Mountaineering Association had provided name and address, or what used to be Mr. Gerrard's address. He had, in fact, skipped off over a year previously - off to Ben Nevis, he had said – owing ten weeks' rent, volunteered his landlord, throwing in a free character reference for good measure.

The other two turned out to be a rather precious pair who had registered at the Fairmont Hotel, Andrew McNee and Gerry Kendall. The Fairmont prided itself on its cuisine and the waiter actually remembered them from fifteen months ago. "Aye, a right bloody nuisance they were. Always scrapping and shouting and sniping at one another. To be perfectly honest with you one of them was not the sort of person we're accustomed to here at the Fairmont. The sort that feels uncomfortable in a hotel like this and reacts by throwing his weight about, finding fault with everything."

Annie later found out that they shared a flat near Macclesfield and had obviously, at that stage, felt the need to falsify their address in the hotel register. They turned out to be partners in an interior design business (pricey decorators, Annie uncharitably assumed). They were thought to be partners in another sense also. There had been the slightest flick off an eyebrow at the "Fairmont" when Dick was informed that they had booked a double room. In Cheshire, they had kept themselves pretty much to themselves and their clients. Nobody had seen either of them since October 1983. They had worked from a lock-up garage and had left its contents and a number of debts behind. They were thought to have jumped just ahead of the bailiff.

Annie would have been quite content to leave all these three to their sordid little lives but for one thing – they all measured up to the description of the body on the Ben.

CHAPTER 7

Annie knew before she even asked what the Super's answer would be and she also knew, as he pointed out, that she should not have asked.

"Come on, now, Annie; you really can't expect the Police Authority to pick up the bills for your own private frolics. You've a wide measure of discretion about how you use your time. You know perfectly well that if you were clear in your own mind that you had to go gadding off to Nottingham and Cheshire you needn't ask me. You're only asking me now because if you asked yourself you'd say 'no' wouldn't you?"

Annie had to agree.

"Well then; come on. Any reason you had to suppose you were on CID business, Fort William business at least, disappeared in Consett, didn't it?"

Annie was not satisfied that there were no criminal aspects to the matter but they were the concern of the Consett CID, not her, and the Super had pre-empted her on that one. She had reported fully to the local police on what she had found before leaving Consett. That was now up to them. She nevertheless still stood there looking, thought the Super, like the only lad on the block without a pair of football boots.

"Look; if the Spean Bridge Rescue want to keep their log tidy, that's no concern of mine, but it's something you'll have to do in your own time, OK? If some Sassenach bobby assumes you're on police business, I won't disabuse him. But that's the best we can do, isn't it?"

And Annie had had to agree; though why, she asked herself, did he always have to be both right and bloody

50

reasonable with it?

She had to wait, therefore, until the following Friday evening before heading off south once again. She had decided to go to Nottingham first. There was no particular reason to suppose that Gerrard would be any easier to eliminate than either of the two "designers" but she was intrigued by the intention, declared in the CIC Hut log, to solo Point Five Gully. October was very early in the season for it to be in good winter condition; she couldn't remember off the cuff what it had been like at that time in 1983. As a rock route, it was hard but uninspiring. Even assuming it had been in decent winter condition, Gerrard had contemplated a very serious undertaking if, that is, his entry in the log was to be taken at face value. The route, 1,000 feet of extremely steep ice, had originally occupied one of the very best ropes in Scotland for no less than five days and even though gear, particularly ice-tools and crampons, had since improved immeasurably, it was still far from a doddle. Only a really competent and experienced team would undertake it – correction, SHOULD undertake it – a couple of idiots who should never have gone near it occasionally ventured on it. Those who might reasonably undertake a solo attempt were unlikely to be pushing fifty as, apparently, was Gerrard. They could be counted on the fingers of one hand, and Annie thought she knew them all. Yet neither she nor any of the Spean Bridge lads had heard of this Gerrard.

She had tried to settle the business on the 'phone. Gerrard had worked at a Poly in South Notts, as a lecturer (predictably, thought Annie to herself, though she could not think why and put it down to prejudice) in sociology. A call to his head of department, however, had yielded the information that he had chucked his job in a year and a half previously, "most inconveniently just after the start of term and just ahead of the boot" Professor Simpson had said. "Christ" thought Annie "not another one, surely. What was it about October, 1983 that was causing all these characters to disappear?"

Nevertheless, she was sure, as she drove south, that she would find some less dramatic explanation for Gerrard's disappearance. She was particularly hopeful of a colleague of Gerrard's at the Poly in the Physics Department who, Gerrard's Head had said, often climbed with Gerrard.

Terry Bates had indeed known Gerrard well, and not just Gerrard the climber. Annie could hardly have asked for better witnesses than he and Professor Ted Simpson, Head of Sociology.

Gerrard was one of those who had found a niche in academic life in the boom which started in the late fifties. He had had a "good" start in life, that is to say, his parents had been able to afford to send him to a second-rate public school, "second-rate" in this context, meaning in contradistinction to third, fourth, and fifth-rate, not, in short, a bad school. There were, however, always some who did not fit and Gerrard had apparently been one of these. The odd thing about second-rate schools was that they only produced "types". First-rate schools produced some "types" but also some individuals. In second-rate schools even the rebels were a "type" or so it seemed to her, mused Annie. Gerrard seemed, from all the signs to have been one of these. He had embraced a "hippy" lifestyle, in so far as it was allowed, in the sixth form and had emerged as one of those spongy, in-principle-rebelling types. If you had ventured the proposition that absolute zero was on the cool side you could have banked on a dissent from Gerrard and you would have been guaranteed a tirade against the antecedents, intelligence and motives of any who thought otherwise.

Following the standard advice, Gerrard had applied for a place in a fifth-grade university just in case all else failed and, all else having failed, had ended up there in a fifth-rate department. Embracing the appropriate clichés with enthusiasm, he had ended up with a mediocre degree. Viewing the ivory tower as a suitable elevation from which to visit his opinions on the rest of mankind and lacking any disposition or vocation for doing anything else, he had contrived first to join the ranks of those on grants from public funds who never completed a thesis and then to swell the ranks of those carrying the sociology gospel to the rising generation in higher education. He would have preferred an Oxford college - where, after all, was the good news more needed than amongst the scions of the privileged? - but had finally decided to live amongst the dispossessed and grasped at the opportunity of an assistant lectureship at the Monkstone College of Higher Education. Having no choice in the matter made the decision easier. A series of moves, some voluntary, had led him to a temporary job at Brideport Poly in his late thirties where his job had finally been made permanent some years later, as a result of an administrative mishap. There, in spite of his best efforts, he had stuck.

There are simple rules for survival in any organisation. It matters not that Gerrard did not understand what they were, for if he had, he would very likely have flouted them. Nevertheless, the course of his life would have been very much smoother if only he had observed rule number one and kept a low profile. Even a high profile is not necessarily disastrous provided it is a homogeneous profile. He could have sniped at his betters with impunity if only his behaviour otherwise had been impeccable. Or he could have indulged his appetites without restraint if only he had combined it with an unctuous sycophancy. Instead, he had committed the cardinal sin of combining conduct for which he stood, quite unfairly, to be punished with conduct, which, equally unfairly, he would otherwise have got away with, with the result that, by mid-1983, he was teetering on the brink of dismissal.

It is not easy to be sacked from higher education. Within two months of arriving at Brideport, however, Gerrard had already embarked on what, with hindsight, appeared to be a determined course designed to achieve this difficult feat. Even relaxed colleagues were faintly embarrassed by the sight of his slightly greying, balding, paunchy figure shouting slogans at the window of the Administrative Block during the statutory occupations of 1968 and then there was the Wang Su Chen affair.

Gerrard had conceived, and who is to say that he was wrong, that too many barriers stand between mentor and *protégé* in the formal classroom situation for any effective exchange of ideas to take place. There may therefore be something to be said for Gerrard's decision to take his tutorials in the Union bar, mutual inhibitions being progressively dissolved by the means there readily available. Except, that is, where the disciple is a serious-minded teetotal Straits Chinese Methodist; and Wang Su Chen feared for his immortal soul every time he came within a hundred yards of a pub. Wang was not bent on trouble making and he was a diligent student.

When tutorials were denied him by Gerrard's scheme for demolishing the barriers, he did not complain. He simply got his head down and did his best. Gerrard would not or could not believe that such a student might deserve to pass an examination. It was not that Wang failed to attend tutorials; refusal to attend could evidence potential, provided it was for the right reasons. Wang's reasons were totally wrong. A mind cluttered as Wang's clearly was by prejudice and preconceptions was by definition incapable of the necessary intellectual development. Gerrard therefore considered a mark off zero to be appropriate.

There is something ineluctably tragic about a man who puts "zero" on a paper when "37" will attain the same objective and attract little comment. Wang, not surprisingly, had complained, his papers had been remarked at an uninspiring "pass" and Gerrard had come within an ace of the chop. He adjusted his behaviour accordingly. He gave up tutorials in the bar transferring them to his room, after dinner, with selected female students.

He should have selected with greater care. There is a fine line between sexual harassment and legitimate "chatting up" and many of us would, no doubt, welcome a more precise definition for the latter is, surely, a desirable social activity. If there is a distinction, it must consist in preserving full freedom of choice and avoiding reasonable offence. It is surprising, however, how many young women otherwise of good taste are capable of being flattered by the attention of an ageing trendy into abandoning all sensibility in these matters. Unfortunately, not all and distinguishing between those susceptible to flattery and those not is crucial. Sadly Gerrard's discrimination was insufficiently refined, otherwise he would not have thrust himself, drunkenly, flies open, at a happily-married 26 year old who had interrupted her career as a nurse in order to qualify herself for even higher things.

This time, nothing could save Gerrard. It is conceivable that had he produced the great, hitherto undiscovered over-arching social science theory he might have been relieved of teaching duties and given a year to seek employment elsewhere. He had, however, never got round to the necessary spadework to put himself in a position to make any substantial contribution to scholarship. Worse, his only appearance in print (a short, if pungent, comment on a recently published work) had led to a charge of plagiarism by a junior colleague who had earlier shown to Gerrard, vainly hoping for useful comment, his draft review of the same work. By the middle of 1983, then, Gerrard had come to think that a change of career might be beneficial.

This was the potted biography of Gerrard that Annie got from Professor Simpson. "So you sacked him, then, did you?" she had then asked.

"Good lord, no. Can't afford to sack people. It takes a committee of seven sitting for about nine months with the alleged offender suspended on full pay. No, we asked him to resign."

"I take it he played the white man, then?"

"Well, six months' pay, superannuation contributions returned and nothing said; much the best thing all round, don't you think?"

"So he wouldn't be entirely penniless when he left, then," calculated Annie.

"Well, he'd have about five and a half months' salary and something like the same amount in returned contributions. No, he'd be able to manage for a while alright," Simpson confirmed.

"What would he do, though," wondered Annie. "Would he get another job or what?"

"Oh, he'd be finished in academic life alright. He was getting on, you know. Even without the scandal – and it's a pretty small world; everybody would know about it – I can't think who'd take him. A bit long in the tooth to pass himself off as a whizz-kid and much too little done to have any credit. Have you spoken to Terry Bates, yet? He'd know a lot more about any plans that Gerrard might have had than I would."

Bates was unable to be more than vague on this point because Gerrard himself had been vague; "I saw him shortly before he left. Actually, he wanted me to go with him – jack it all in and go and do our own thing, that sort of thing, but I told him I thought he was past that and he certainly was."

Annie was getting a bit lost. "Go where; do what? Did he say what he had in mind?"

"Oh, the mountain thing – wanted to go off and potter about. Do all the climbs he'd only dreamed about. Visit other ranges, Andes, Himalayas, etcetera."

"But what did he intend to live on?"

"Well, they treated him quite generously, you know. So he had a bit of a cushion to start. Anyway, you can manage, can't you; social security and the odd bit of black work. A bit old for the mountain bum scenario, I thought – about a quarter of a century too old," Bates chuckled "but he didn't. Anyway, that was what he called his 'fall-back' position. He had ideas about qualifying as a guide. That was quite ludicrous. Fancied himself as a climbing journalist. Trouble was, he was just a run-of-the-mill climber. To be honest, he hadn't actually done very much. Really hadn't been anywhere. He was the sort who talks more than he climbs, and who climbs for the beer and the girls – you know the sort."

Annie did indeed know the sort. "But he had no reputation did he? I mean I've never heard of him."

"Oh no. But he was going to change all that.

Annie wondered exactly how.

"I saw him just before he left. That's when he asked me to go with him but as I say, it struck me as zany. No, his idea was to 'arouse the whole climbing establishment with a series of remarkable solo climbs.' That was exactly how he put it. I told him he was mad."

"But from what you say, he was nowhere near up to it. As well, I would have thought, as being long past it. Didn't you try and talk him out of it? He'd likely kill himself, wouldn't he?" Annie realised, with some embarrassment, that she had waxed slightly sanctimonious.

"Well, to be honest, I didn't take him seriously. He was a bit of the 'all-mouth-and-no-trousers' sort. I can just about imagine him getting to the start of Point Five Gully, but not any further."

"Was Point Five on his list for a solo ascent, then?"

"Oh, yes. At he top of it. That's what he headed off to do when he left, or so he told me."

All this boiled down to very little more than confirming what Annie had already speculated when Dick first told her about the pretentious entry in the CIC Hut logbook. It took her no further down the road. Neither Simpson nor Bates had heard anything of Gerrard since he had set off for the Ben. Bates speculated that he would have gone off to the Alps or Pyrenees; possibly the Himalayas. An item on his agenda had been a protracted stay in the latter – a year or two trekking or climbing. Research, he'd called it, for the classic work on the range.

Possibly that was what he had done. Annie decided to put the word about to try and find out if anyone had run across him. The Himalayan climbing scene was a small world and, if he had gone there, there was a fair chance news would filter back. She had a sneaking feeling, however, that this was just going through the motions. There was more than something simply odd about this whole business. It now looked as though four or possibly five people who had been on the Ben during this short period had disappeared without trace. It was much more than odd. It was supernatural; she felt the hairs on the back of her head standing up.

CHAPTER 8

It was in a mood of distrusting the obvious and expecting the improbable that Annie left Nottinghamshire. Gerrard had headed off from Nottinghamshire apparently for Ben Nevis and nothing whatever had been heard of him since. She appreciated rationally that it was likely he who had come to grief on the Ben fifteen months previously. He had been no Hilary; even in October the north face was capable of taxing a really able climber. If Bates was a reliable judge, Gerrard was not that. Gerrard had, however, been the fourth "suspect" and the other three (Piper, Jenkinson and Welsby) had all turned out to have "alibis" when it came to the crunch. Although, therefore, common sense told her that clearing up the puzzle of the two missing Cheshire designers should be a formal matter, she reserved judgment.

The night spent at an old-world pub in Hathersage reminded her with pleasure of visits to the gritstone edges and limestone crags of Derbyshire more years ago than she cared to remember. Early the following morning, she was on the road again, heading for Macclesfield where "Kendall & McNee" had carried on business as "Interior decorators". The brusque simplicity of the firm's name had surprised her. She had anticipated "Stylistique" or "Moderna Design" or some such, run by a couple of mincing ponces who exaggerated every gesture. Odd how persistent such stereotypes and prejudiced language were. She had known a lot of "gays" (she still paused briefly before she used the term) and hardly any had conformed to the model, yet it remained the image conjured up in her mind whenever the topic arose.

From the little she was able to glean in Macclesfield, neither Gerry Kendall nor Andrew McNee conformed to the stereotype either. McNee especially seemed to have been a totally different type. A solid, surly, unimaginative decorator from Manchester, he had not gone down at all well among the nouveau riche of Prestbury, two miles up the road where the firm had found most of its business. In his personality lay the probable explanation not only for the name but also for the failure of the business, thought Annie.

Kendall was a different kettle of fish. He had, apparently, been a passive, sensitive even delicate flower. He appeared to have a genuine love of beautiful things though few had turned up amongst the possessions impounded by the owner of the lock-up garage from which the firm had carried on business. Presumably he had not been able to afford them at all events from his own resources. No doubt spending clients' money on them was his sublimation. From the piles of magazines left behind it appeared that he had gratified his tastes at one remove. The neighbours and business acquaintances to whom Annie spoke based their speculations about the homosexual nature of the relationship upon Kendall's persona rather than McNee's. Even so, Kendall had been shy and retiring rather than extrovert and obviously gay.

No-one in the Macclesfield area knew them well and Annie was able to glean only a superficial understanding of their characters and relationship. It happened, however, that one of their clients was the owner of a Manchester club which the pair frequented. That was, indeed, why they got the job of "improving" to her tastes the desirable Prestbury residence which his wife had goaded him into buying. The club, it turned out, was much frequented by local gays some of whom were able to provide Annie with a more detailed portrait of the Macclesfield pair.

No-one knew exactly how long they had been together but it was a period of some years. It seemed, however, clear that by October 1983 the relationship had ceased to be either easy or happy. It seemed originally to have been a case of unlike poles attracting. McNee, five years the older of the two, bore a constant resentment. He could well have been one of those older gays who never wholly reconcile themselves to their sexuality but instead harbour a constant internal conflict between two opposing emotional pulls. Half of McNee appeared to wish to repudiate his sexual inclination and irrationally blamed Kendall for it. On top of this resentment were piled two others. McNee was as promiscuous as opportunity allowed him to be. Kendall had been possessive and wore a constant air of reproach. McNee hated him for that and even more for his weakness and ineptitude in the mountains.

The mountaineering interest came exclusively from McNee. He had been yet another of those South Lancashire tradesmen who had escaped from the grime of that most unattractive of conurbations to the peace and challenge of the hills. It was probably the only thing that he ever really cared about and he had no intention of abandoning his interest merely because he had become attached to an aesthetic wimp. He had made his compromise. He had ground a perfectly adequate living out of his one-man painting and decoration business and had only very reluctantly, at Kendall's insistence gone upmarket into the interior design business. Kendall owed him the outdoors at weekends and holidays. He paid however only reluctantly and infrequently.

If you had asked Kendall, he would have insisted that the headaches, stomach upsets and bad back were perfectly genuine but no proof would have satisfied McNee. He would not even concede hypochondria. In fact, both were right up to a point. At first, Kendall had made genuine efforts to share his partner's enthusiasm but, try as he might, he could derive no pleasure from the cold, damp, breathless slogs up onto a misty plateau. It was worse when it came to climbing. He had neither skill nor strength but he did have imagination and every moment of every climb the two ever did was filled with terror. No care or assurance by McNee could abate it. His first pleas of illness were, as McNee suspected, totally phoney and a means only of avoiding yet another day of misery. More recently, however, he had seemed to be contracting every small ailment that was doing the rounds. He was never well but he had cried "wolf" too often and McNee would have none of it.

The last news of the two at the start of October 1983 caused Annie to wonder why they were still together. On the occasion of their last appearance at the club, their behaviour had acutely embarrassed their few acquaintances. Business was bad. Kendall had spent much of the evening in tearful recrimination at McNee for his latest infidelity and furthermore had claimed and appeared to be distinctly unwell. McNee was having none of it. He asked little enough of Kendall, he insisted, and if Kendall couldn't bring himself to accompany him for a few days in Scotland, that merely showed how little Kendall really cared for him. The air of the Highlands would do him a power of good. For some reason Kendall just wanted to make a mess of his, McNee's life. He had ruined his business but he wasn't going to take away his great joy in life. McNee was going whether Kendall liked it or not. And if he didn't like it, he could go his own way. He, McNee would be a damned sight better off without him... and so it had gone on.

It had ended dramatically for the onlookers. McNee had stomped off out of the club and that was the last any had seen of him. The continued presence of the deserted Kendall had put a real damper on the evening. A couple of the others had eventually given him a lift home. He had not been seen since either.

The visit to Macclesfield and Manchester had yielded little more than could be inferred from Dick's inquiries at the Fairmont Hotel, Annie admitted to herself as she drove back north. Come to think of it, it would have made sense for her to ensure that this particular vein had been exhausted before she set off south but it would have meant a delay of a week. She resolved, however, that it would be her first port of call on her return. She found out little more. They had turned up at the Fairmont - they had not booked – on the third day before they had skipped off. Few details had fixed themselves in memory so firmly as to survive the intervening fifteen months but they had been unpopular guests. "That sort" was not welcome; other guests had been embarrassed. If they had kept themselves to themselves that would not have been so bad but they would insist on making their quarrels public. They had had a row at breakfast on the second day and the older one, the coarse one, had gone off for the day on his own. He'd been wholly unreasonable. The other one was obviously not at all well. He had spent the day in their room, hadn't come down for lunch and had eaten practically nothing at dinner. On the third day, the older one ("McNee that would be" offered Annie) had been even worse. He had bullied the sick one unmercifully at breakfast and eventually they had gone off together, geared up for the mountains though the younger one would have been better off in hospital. What had happened to them goodness only knows. In a good hotel you didn't ask for payment in advance but then you didn't expect "people like that" either.

A pile of paperwork ("it was incredible how quickly it accumulated and to how little purpose" Annie had commented to herself) had kept her at the station until seven that evening. She had picked up fish and chips on the way home, lit a log fire and settled down in front of the second-hand, black-and-white television set. There were times when she could watch anything but this was not one of them. Her eyes were on the screen but her mind was elsewhere. The whole business had become ridiculously complicated. She could hardly believe that she now had three more candidates for title to the body on the Ben. Kendall seemed much the likeliest of these but she couldn't rule out McNee either. If the normal rules of the game had applied, the most probable explanation would be that these two had both come to grief and she wondered if another body was up there awaiting discovery. The extreme unlikelihood that two bodies had been up there all this time undiscovered rather ruled out a double tragedy in the case of Kendall and McNee. Gerrard was surely the front-runner.

But all this was premature. Her investigation had necessarily been superficial notwithstanding that she had lavished more time and trouble on it than the Super thought justifiable. A really thorough and determined assault on the problem would almost certainly account for all three. It remained unsettling, however, that so many who were on the Ben at that time were proving so hard to trace. And even if this latest three all subsequently turned up in some remote corner of the globe where was she then? In her eight years with the Spean Bridge Rescue she had brought down many broken bodies down off the mountains but it had been rare for there to be a problem of identification. Even on the few occasions when this had been the case she could recall not a single one in which they had not got it right first time. In this case she had already ruled out several possibilities yet now found herself sitting there contemplating three more. But that wasn't the worst of it. Her inquiries had acquainted her with the lives of nine people in all, not forgetting Rosemary Jenkinson. Nine people and she had discovered the whereabouts of not a single one of them. It was time to stop, think and go over the ground again. She must have got something wrong, somewhere along the way. What was it?

CHAPTER 9

Annie had done her best to wind down. She had washed her hair and soaked in a hot bath for over half an hour. She had carried out a personal inventory in the privacy of her bedroom and had been gratified to note that she really was wearing quite well. As the thirties progressed you became more and more conscious of the likelihood of imminent disintegration but she still looked pretty good. She easily kept fit and there was not an ounce of spare fat on her. Her belly was as flat as it had been when she was a teenager and her tits, she reckoned, would still pass the pencil test.

Although it was not yet eleven o'clock she was now sitting up in bed, a pint mug of cocoa steaming on the table alongside her, clipboard and pencil in hand. On it, she had so far written:

"1. 19-year old. Still missing? Where last seen, witnesses? Premature senility?!"

That he had been nineteen and the body estimated to be at least thirty years older had seemed rather a clincher. She was not, however, going to miss a trick this time. There was the disease or condition she had vaguely heard of. She half-remembered extreme cases of 9-year olds with all the appearance of being 70. She was certainly, however, going to spend half an hour with the ENCYCLOPAEDIA OF FORENSIC SCIENCE AND MEDICAL TOXICOLOGY before she considered broaching the topic with Dr. Kenny. He terrified her even when she asked him the time of day. He'd crucify her if she came up with a suggestion like this unless she had made bloody sure of her ground. If she could possibly avoid it, she would do so. The note continued:

"Bottom priority."

"2. Sandy Piper – right age, size, build etc. Munro-bagger, likely candidate but eleven months too soon… not necessarily! Could have been elsewhere for eleven months. Who reported him missing? Dark lady across the border. Who was she? Piper shacked up with her. Why so secretive?"

"Distinctly possible but no connection with others. Does this matter?"

This last note had surprised her slightly. It forced her to admit openly to herself that she was not going to rest content merely with putting a name to the corpse in Glover's Chimney. She had remarked on previous occasions that you could tell yourself things you otherwise wouldn't hear by writing them down.

"3. Rosemary Jenkinson. Clearly not – wrong sex – Chronic transvestite?"

"This is getting ridiculous," thought Annie. Rosemary had spent almost her whole life in and around Consett. It was impossible for her to have kept up such a pretence. Even if not, it was stretching coincidence too far for Arthur to have manifested, late in life, the same highly unusual predilection that Edward would have had to enjoy all his life. Transsexual then? Hardly – that sort of surgery had not yet reached such a degree of perfection as to fool Dr. Kenny. She had wondered briefly whether to bracket Rosemary with the 19-year old and had finally written:

"Impossible… almost."

Next, she had written:

"4. Edward Jenkinson – strong contender, age, sex,

height, build-wise. Anorak business very telling."

She had then written "'Alibi'?" It was several minutes before she added "not at all conclusive."

She really had been rather sloppy. She had not entirely taken the bank people at their word. She had asked if it had been a joint account. The bank had confirmed that it was and that either Edward or Rosemary could draw. But who had drawn the cheques, she had asked. Rosemary, it turned out, had drawn one at the start but thereafter they had all borne Edward's signature. Now Annie wondered if "signature" should be in inverted commas. Forgeries almost always came to light because somebody was defrauded as a result but who would that have been in this case? After the initial hiatus – the overdrawing etc., the account had been put into credit again as a result of dividends being paid in direct by the companies in question. So the bank had not lost. Rosemary might possibly have complained but it looked as though she was a party to whatever conspiracy there was and if she had wanted to disappear she would hardly have been likely to dive into a pool of publicity over a forgery allegation. Edward's entry was therefore subscribed:

"Distinctly possible."

But the question remained, if the signature had been forged, who had forged it? Rosemary had not needed to – she could have drawn over her own signature. The likeliest candidate was Arthur Welsby but he had left Consett with the equivalent of a small fortune in cash and drafts in his sac, all legally his even if somewhat dubiously obtained. Would he really be likely to put himself in peril of a prosecution just to add an illicit penny or two more? Annie thought not. And if he was not the forger, who else could there be?

What, then, about Arthur?

"Arthur Welsby – plate in leg."

Annie had sent her mind down many lanes over this but they were all dead ends. Dr. Kenny would not have missed it and even if he had, he would certainly have checked after her call. Perhaps Agnes had been mistaken; the hospital records would tell. She must exhaust this possibility but Agnes had been absolutely certain. Perhaps "Arthur" was not Arthur but some doppelganger or impersonator. This was getting silly. Even in that extremely unlikely event, Agnes would have known. But would she have said? There was, Annie felt in her bones, something not quite right about Agnes but she couldn't put her finger on it. She would have to come back to that. In the meantime, Arthur's entry earned the comment:

"Very unlikely."

Entries recalling what she had just recently discovered about Gerrard, McNee and Kendall followed. They were all distinctly possible – Gerrard, Kendall and McNee in that order. She regarded Gerrard as favourite but she had not yet made a serious attempt to rule any of them out. This task must obviously be an early one. With any luck she would be able to cross them all off. It really was a bit much to end up with three "possibles" and four "likelys" on her clipboard. There was, after all, only the one body.

Annie put down the board, drained the last of her cocoa, now cold, switched off the bedside light and turned over to sleep. The *dramatis personae* of the affair were flitting about darkly on the ill-lit stage of her mind. It was Agnes, however, who kept thrusting herself into sharper focus. What was it about Agnes that nagged at her? There was something incongruous about the portrait of Agnes that had been painted for her, something that didn't quite fit. She strove to put the finger of her mind on it but had begun to remark recently that as you grew older the more you tried the more what you wanted slipped out of reach. She literally gave up – for a couple of minutes her mind toyed with other things. Then, suddenly, she sat up.

She had it! It was, though, a bit of an anti-climax. Not quite the sort of revelation associated with the Road to Damascus and she felt a little disappointed. There it was, however, for what it was worth. Agnes had presented herself to Annie as being thoroughly unworldly and subservient to Arthur where money matters were concerned. Yet except for one building society account which was in Agnes's name, all their investments were in joint names. Arthur had not come across as an egalitarian or lovey-dovey type but most of their small fortune had been inherited by him. Why had he decided to incur the inconvenience of having to have all transactions executed by both? More – what was it that she had been told about Agnes? She was the sort who counted every penny, who kept close tabs on everything? Was this the sort of person who would blindly sign anything stuck under her nose by a weak character like Arthur? And if she wasn't, would Arthur risk the whole venture by trying to dupe her into signing? It seemed unlikely. Annie was going to have to pay another visit to Consett. There went another of her precious weekends.

She turned over again and this time slept. She drove to work the following morning going over it all again and compiling an exhaustive mental list of what had to be cleared up when she went back to Consett. It was well into the afternoon before she began to think that maybe the Consett trip would not be needed after all. That was the result of Tom McIntyre walking into her office.

CHAPTER 10

When Dick had taken his afternoon stroll up to the CIC Hut to inspect the logbook he had discovered the names of several who were up there at or about the crucial time. Most were local lads or at least regulars known to the Spean Bridge lot and all but two had been readily eliminated. They had had nothing out of the ordinary to report.

The two were Ken Gerrard and the Edinburgh advocate, Tom McIntyre. Dick had tried to contact McIntyre via his Edinburgh chambers but he had been in court. Dick had explained the nature of his enquiries to McIntyre's clerk who had promised to pass the matter on. He had undertaken that if McIntyre had any information that might be helpful he would be in touch.

When he had heard nothing either that day or the next Dick had crossed McIntyre off just like all the others. The clerk had faithfully passed on Dick's message. McIntyre had had some information which might or might not be helpful. He didn't know. He was now belatedly getting touch. He had promised himself a few days in Glencoe as soon as he could get clear and had only now managed to do so. It had not struck him that there was anything compelling or urgent about identifying a corpse which had already been on the mountain for fifteen months. And anyway he was an inefficient and, in all things that didn't much matter, a chronic procrastinator.

He and Annie had been friends for a number of years and had climbed together on numerous occasions. Annie knew well that to Tom mountains were among the things that mattered and that where they were concerned he was neither idle nor inefficient. He was one of the safest men she knew. He had not always been so but experience in the form of a bitter night spent out on the Buchaille with a broken leg had taught him that to be safe you had to take precautions not only against the dangers you could foresee but also against those you couldn't.

Annie liked him. She had sometimes wondered her interest in him might not be greater than that and had him filed away in her mind as one of the few men she genuinely regarded as marriageable though without any wish to place herself on the list of candidates for the eligible bachelor. Asked why not when debating the perennial topic of men friends with an intimate at her flat one night she had replied "because I know him too well" and had often since then tried to explain to herself what she meant by that.

They were always delighted to see one another. They were so now despite the immediate cause of their latest meeting. He grabbed her by the shoulders and solemnly placed a kiss on each cheek and one on her forehead and intoned, with solemnity, *"Un pour toi, un pour moi et un pour le bon Dieu."* They exchanged malicious gossip about mutual friends and Annie insisted on cooking for him that evening, an invitation which he accepted with a mockingly ungracious but not wholly unwarranted "if I must." Then he interrupted the easy flow of the banter with:

"Look, let's get this damned business out of the way, then we can get down to more pleasurable things." And what might they be, wondered Annie.

She had concurred, he had said "right" and he had given her a monologue, comprehensive of all the relevant facts and warrantable inferences, sequential, impeccably logical and almost totally lacking in those nuances and speculations which fleshed the bones of actual real-life events.

"I only finally got away from Edinburgh at about 5.30 p.m. Bloody annoying, actually, but some consultation that I'd thought would last about half an hour went on and on. Can't remember what case it was; doesn't matter. I got to the car park about nine and belted up to the Hut as quickly as I could in the dark. It's about time something was done about that wretched path. It's like trying to dance in treacle at the bottom end. Got to the hut at about half past ten. About half a dozen blokes there, as I recall.

Annie interrupted. "Can you remember who they were? Did you know them?"

Tom named three whom he knew well and continued:

"I'd seen a couple of the others before as well. Can't remember their names. There was one bloke I hadn't seen before; English, northerner, middle-aged being charitable, middle fifties, I'd say. Tell you about him later. Anyway, I was knackered and turned in pretty-well straight away. Fancied some solitude on Observatory Ridge for the morrow.

"Saw this English bloke briefly the following morning. Others had gone off earlier for something on Carn Dearg Buttress I think. Asked him what he had in mind – making conversation sort of thing. He replied 'thinking of Point Five. Fancy it?' Nearly burst out laughing but controlled myself and told him 'a bit much for me, I'm afraid'."

Annie chuckled. They had done the route together a couple of years back. It had been in prime condition – never easier – yet they had had a real tussle with it and now chorused, whenever it was mentioned, 'a bit much for me, I'm afraid'.

"He went off and I geared up and followed, oh, fifteen minutes, twenty minutes later. Saw him next on Tower Ridge. Changed his mind, obviously! Anyway, you want to know who went down Glover's Chimney, right? Well, could have been he. I'd gone for Observatory Ridge, as planned. You know how the route wanders a bit, mostly on the right but occasionally on the left. Could easily see progress on Tower Ridge when I was on the right, of course and picked him out now and again.

"I'd seen him first at the initial chimney. Made a real ballsup of an attempt to rope it solo; got himself all tangled up. He got up alright eventually but obviously abandoned the roping. Coiled it and slung it over his sac again.

"Anyway, I next saw him reaching the Gap. Hands and knees, crouching, you know. Took a longish time at the Gap. Lowered himself over but couldn't make up his mind to lean across. Last I saw of him; could well be your man."

"But you didn't see him go?" queried Annie.

"No. I said 'could have been your man' didn't I?"

"Is that all?" A hint of exasperation tinged Annie's voice.

"No, it isn't'. There's more. Thought I'd give you a complete run-down but if you just want selected snippets, say so."

"Sorry, no. Carry on. Can you remember what he was wearing?" asked Annie, remembering the anorak.

"Not very clearly, I'm afraid. Obviously, nothing particularly remarkable."

"Sweater, cagoule, jacket, anorak," prompted Annie.

"An anorak; a newish one, I think. Could have been black with some red, as I recall."

So it could have been THE anorak thought Annie. It partly fitted the description, but then so did about a million others anoraks.

"What about gear? You say he started off trying to rope solo. He'd be wearing a harness would he," prompted Annie.

"Had a harness on when he left the hut. Rope slung across the top of his sac. All I can tell you, I'm afraid."

"That's it then, is it?" checked Annie.

"No it isn't. Hold your horses. That's suspect number one. There was another lot."

"You mean another party on the Ridge... Tower Ridge?"

"Yes," he went on. "A pair. Didn't see them until I was higher up, near the top. They were at the Gap. Must have been having some sort of row; must have been a hell of a row to carry across to me. One stuck on one side of the Gap, the other leaping up and down (metaphorically, not literally) on the summit side, trying to get the first one across." Annie was about to interrupt. He wouldn't let her but pressed on. "Leaper then stops leaping, solemnly unties, throws the rope at the other and sets off for the summit tower."

"Christ Almighty," swore Annie. "Just left him, like that?"

"Yup. Well, that was the last I saw. I watched for a minute or so. Seemed there ought to be something I should do. Thought about yelling. Decided I'd give the bloke a piece of my mind if I saw him on the summit plateau. Decided I'd descend via Tower Ridge whether I saw him or not."

"Did you?"

"What, see him, or descend via Tower Ridge? Answer to the second is 'yes' and to the first 'don't know'."

"What do you mean, 'don't know'?"

"Saw a couple of blokes on top. Don't know that he was either. I couldn't actually recognise him on the Ridge, you know. Nobody I knew, so far as I am aware. I was a fair bit away. Could have been either of 'em. Both a bit sullen, evasive even. One of them had obviously walked up from Fort William – still in his city gear and brand-new anorak. Saw the other one again later when I was heading off down. Shot off to the Fort like his arse was on fire."

Annie thought about what he had told her. "Well, that seems an altogether more likely set-up doesn't it. Could well have been the body of the bloke left behind, trying to get himself down, do you think?"

"Or the other one, trying to get back to him," pointed out Tom.

Annie, duly corrected agreed. Then "did you go back down via the Ridge?"

"Yup. Never done it before. Quite interesting."

"See anything, anybody?"

"Nope. Looked around the Gap. Nothing. Passed another couple on the way up. Bit late, I thought, you might be here for the night. Otherwise, nothing. In a bit of a hurry, actually."

"Well, many thanks," she now conceded to Tom. He interrupted her.

"That's all I can offer you on the Glover's Chimney business."

"Why; do you think there's something else I might be

interested in?"

"It's just that there was something going on at the bottom of Tower Gully, as well. Just thought I'd mention it. I was coming down off the summit, heading for the Ridge. Heard a bit of commotion at the bottom of the Gully and realised that some bloke had fallen. Saw him come to rest. No idea how far he'd fallen but the likeliest thing was a trip going down the Gully, which would be unlikely to do a lot of harm. Then it occurred to me that it might be the poor sod who'd been abandoned at the Gap in which case, it could be extremely serious. Thought "Christ; it's all happening today." Thought I was going to have to get down to see to him but I spotted a couple of other blokes heading for him, one from above, one from below. Expected to hear all about it at the bottom at the Hut later but nothing. Can't have been badly hurt. They must have got him off and down without too much trouble. No mention of it in the Fort that evening so I reckoned it must have had a happy ending. Just thought I'd mention it."

"Glad you did," said Annie, wishing he hadn't.

CHAPTER 11

A Return to Consett

When she came to think about it Annie came to the conclusion that Tom's evidence had merely reshuffled the possibilities.

She now knew, for sure, that Gerrard belonged on her list. It was a hard fact that he had gone for Tower Ridge. Tom had seen him on it. Correction – in so far as it was possible to ascertain the fact by observation from Observatory Ridge, Gerrard had been on Tower Ridge. That was not quite the same thing.

If, however, Tom's observations had been accurate then Gerrard had certainly been in a position to qualify for title to the corpse in Glover's Chimney. Annie could imagine him, hesitating about taking that fateful and possibly fatal step across the Gap. It was impossible to escape that moment when you were committed, when you leaned over to rest yourself against the far wall before stepping over and getting your hands on the jug-handle holds that pulled you up to security. Once you decided to go there was no revoking the decision and, if you were that crucial bit off balance, you would end up not leaning against the far wall but against thin air. She had no difficulty conjuring up the picture of Gerrard finally steeling himself, leaning out and then realizing, too late, that he hadn't quite got it right, that he was off balance, scrabbling unavailingly, then accelerating sac and all then head torn off before being brought to a crushing halt in the cleft where the body was found.

"Christ," she pulled herself up. "It just isn't a difficult

move. Even if he did do most of his climbing with his mouth it was at the very least improbable that he would come to grief like that." She turned her thoughts to the other pair.

From what she had learned about Kendall and McNee in Macclesfield and Manchester tacked onto what had been reported about the breakfast quarrel at the Fairmont on the morning of the last day on which either had been seen, it could well be they. At least, what Tom had observed chimed very nicely with the picture of the pair which had emerged. If it were they and if Kendall had been deserted and left to his own devices on the far side of the Gap, he had to be a strong contender. He appeared to have had negligible experience of such a situation and even less nous about how to extricate himself from it. Annie tried to put herself in his place – to face the problem as he had had to. What would she have done?

There was little to choose between going on and going back. Kendall (if it were he) had the rope. If he had had the wit to think, coolly, about his problem, he could have protected himself for the step across the Gap quite easily. That would have required no great experience. And once across the Gap, even he could have coped with the rest, the simple scree-scramble to and then up the summit tower, then the broad highway down to Fort William. Equally, the rope could have guaranteed him a safe if more complicated and time-consuming descent of the Ridge. Most of the way, it varied between a walk and an easy scramble. There were only one or two places where the added security of the rope would even need to be considered and, again, anyone with a modicum of common sense would have contrived a way to use it. McNee was the one who lacked any protection.

The trouble was there seemed to be little evidence that Kendall was in a state to summon any of the common-sense he might have mustered in less trying circumstances. It was, Annie had to admit to herself, by no means unlikely that Kendall would think in terms of trying to take the shortest way off that abominable ridge and try to scramble down to Tower Gully or, via Glover's Chimney, in the Number Two Gully direction. Or he could, bearing in mind the state he was in, simply have blundered off, anyhow, anywhere. Anyone would have to admit that he was the strongest contender for the title. He would, indeed, have seemed a certainty to Annie except that he might just have stayed there, frozen with terror, until the hysteria passed, until, drained even of the emotion to fuel fear, he picked his way down.

That McNee had left Kendall (assuming it to have been they, and this was not certain, Annie reminded herself) tied onto the rope troubled her momentarily. Then she realized that he could easily have untied in order to try to arrange protection, or rope himself down.

Finally, she had to remember as Tom had reminded her, that McNee himself could not be ruled out. There was no evidence that his abandonment of Kendall was other than short-lived. He might even have taken a plunge from the far side of the Gap before he even had time for recantation – the poor man's equivalent of tripping over your crampons on the easy descent after conquering the Eiger Nordwand, an actual happening, she recalled. If he had taken pity on Kendall he would have had to re-cross the Gap unprotected (unless Kendall, with the rope, helped – not all that likely in the circumstances, she thought). That could be awkward; it might have been catastrophic for McNee.

When Tom had presented himself with evidence of the events which took place on that fateful day Annie had allowed herself to think that her troubles might be over. Instead, she was right back at square one.

Her mind returned to the Consett bunch. There was still a lot to be explained there, even if it turned out to have nothing to do with Ben Nevis. She was on duty the coming weekend so that was not on.   And the weekend after that, she really had to get some rescue practice and training in. She had missed the last one and a deputy leader could hardly skip two in a row. So that ruled that out. She mentally pencilled in the third weekend for a trip south and left it at that.

It was at the rescue practice that she heard the news of Gerrard's possible appearance in the Himalayas if, that is, the news that had percolated back to one of the Spean Bridge lads was to be believed. Gerrard had allegedly been seen by one of his own Notts club mates on an expedition the previous spring. It sounded kosher but she was taking nothing for granted. She decided to knock off Consett and Nottingham in the one trip. That would take more than two days so she tacked a couple of days leave onto her weekend. If she ended up with time to spare she would see a bit more of the Dales on the way back.

She easily made Nottingham in the day and met Don Henshaw, the witness that might enable her to rule out Ken Gerrard, in the pub as arranged on the 'phone. She realized when she saw him that she had met him already but the exact occasion slipped her memory and asking didn't seem to suit her detective image. Don had been one off a party of young Notts climbers who had gone off to the Himalayas to attempt a new route on Satopanth. Strange that Nottinghamshire should be such a strong mountaineering county, thought Annie. Was there anything there other than a couple of worked out quarries. Perhaps it was the lack of any elevation more significant than a coal-tip which drove them all off to hills elsewhere.

She had a very pleasant evening with Don. Bless him; he didn't try to chat her up. Or perhaps he thought her too old for him! His evidence was curt and to the point. He knew Gerrard very well by sight. They belonged to the same club and saw one another almost every Wednesday night at the "Anchor" where the club met. They had hardly ever exchanged a word, however. Don had reckoned he was probably the wrong age, or perhaps the wrong sex, for that. The younger lads were into extreme routes and tended to keep themselves pretty much to themselves. He was aware of Gerrard more because of the latter's interest in women than for any other reason. Gerrard had seemed to be permanently on heat and apparently worked on the principle that if you asked enough women one would take you up. Don couldn't quite see that. Even the monkey on the typewriter would eventually produce the works of Shakespeare only if it had phenomenal stamina. Gerrard, he thought was a bit obviously raddled and past it. But then, it wasn't what he thought that counted, was it?

As for the encounter in the Himalayas, Don was in absolutely no doubt about it. It was in May 1984. They were on their way in. Gerrard had been at the roadhead. Don had said "Hello, Ken. What are you doing here?" Gerrard had immediately turned around and walked away. "And fuck you too," Don had muttered to himself. Gerrard had always been a standoffish bastard but this took the cake.

Annie spent the night in Nottingham and headed off early on the Sunday morning for Consett. She cut over to the M1 and indulged herself with a drive through the Dales, heading off through Otley and Ilkley and then taking the Upper Wharfdale road. She had half a mind to stop in Kettlewell and refresh herself with a walk over Great Whernside and Buckden Pike but it was a grey Dales day and the temptation was easy to resist. Then she remembered a restaurant run by friends near Hawes and decided instead to indulge herself with one of Kate's delicious dinners at Burnsett Hall. Driving up Langstrothdale, the weather improved so she stopped at Bardale Head and knocked off Dodd Fell and Drumaldrace, heading West, then East along the Cam Road.

At Burnsett Hall, she drank too much. You could hardly avoid it. Willy hadn't seen her for ages and immediately opened a bottle of champagne. They had traded awful limericks until turning in at 2 a.m. The Caesar's wife criterion made it impossible for her to drink and drive and that had been justification enough for staying over. She could barely face the scrambled eggs and smoked salmon proffered for breakfast and it was after ten the following morning before she set off again, via Buttertubs, the Stang and Egglestone Common, to Consett.

It had been a mistake, she had decided, to give Agnes notice of her previous visit. Courtesy did not pay. This time she deliberately took Agnes by surprise. Even so, it took considerable time and effort, not easy in the circumstances, to drag the truth out of Agnes. Agnes had not invited her in but had tried to force Annie to settle any business she had in mind on the doorstep. Annie was encouraged to think that Agnes had something to hide but, after inviting herself in, wondered if perhaps it was the pre-lunch brandy Agnes had poured for herself. Can't be wholly on her beam-ends if she can afford to indulge that taste, thought Annie.

Driving over the tops, Annie had wondered where to start. She had decided to bluff with another black truth and after some inconsequential preliminaries stated:

"I'm afraid, Mrs. Welsby, that some questions have arisen about the transfers that you and your husband executed before he left."

It was a direct hit. Agnes was plainly agitated. She was, however, giving nothing away and asked, simply, "Oh really; why. What's the matter?"

"There appears to be some doubt about the authenticity of the signatures." (Another black truth, this. There was some doubt but only in Annie's mind and very speculative it was too. Agnes still wasn't budging.)

"I don't understand what you mean. They were signed by my husband and I. That's correct, isn't it?"

They could go on all day, trading questions like this, thought Annie. She settled on a direct assault.

"Mrs. Welsby; you didn't sign those transfers, did you?"

It was the sort of plain and unambiguous question which has to be answered unhesitatingly and confidently. Quickly as the computer, which is the brain operates, it nevertheless took vital microseconds for Agnes to flip through the various permutations before temporising. "I'm afraid I don't understand what you're getting at. We both signed the transfers." Even then she could have got away with it had she had the emotional stamina to tolerate the silence which

86

ensued. She hadn't. In a now barely audible tone she continued, "No, you're right. I didn't sign them."

So that was established. There remained the question why Agnes had insisted that she had signed and why she had done nothing about the fraud that was now affirmed and which had reduced her station from one of considerable comfort to one of such limited self-indulgence as pre-lunch cognacs. Her explanation lacked conviction but Annie could not budge her from it. She had loved Arthur and could not accept, at first, that he had deserted her. Anyway, it had not dawned on her for some weeks that he had not only deserted her but had also robbed her. She had hardly left the house for three whole days after he left. Annie could check that – ask the neighbours, etc., if anybody had seen her. When she had had to make social contacts once again she had concocted the story that Arthur had got a better job in the South and she was waiting to join him. Annie could check that too. She hadn't known what to do. By the time the awful truth had dawned, it was too late to change her story. Annie would not be able to understand what it was like to be a woman in her position in such a small, isolated community such as Consett. (Oh yes I can, thought Annie who had had to adjust somewhat painfully to life in Fort William.)

Back once again at the "Cross Keys" for a beer and a sandwich Annie tried to imagine what the true explanation for Agnes's silence could be. She did not accept for one moment the image of Agnes as a retiring, vulnerable, wounded little woman. She remembered the bitterness of Agnes's tone on the occasion of their last meeting when Agnes had prematurely voiced her belief that it was her husband who had come to grief on the Ben. That was no loving wife grieving a loss. It was a woman scorned and cheated and then denied even vengeance. Yet Arthur's death would not deny her vengeance by any means. Edward or Rosemary or both had been parties to a criminal conspiracy which had robbed her not only of her husband but also of her wealth. Annie could imagine and believe in an Agnes venturing into the Consett police station and, perplexed, explaining that her husband and his friends seemed to have run off with her money. She had no difficulty imagining the vicious, silent pleasure Agnes would derive from their prosecution and conviction, whether or not this resulted in her fortune being restored. Yet she had done nothing. She had sat and seethed in her mock-Tudor detachment for fifteen months.

The explanation struck Annie quite suddenly. Of course, Annie was herself involved. The bitterness was the child of frustration and the frustration arose because Agnes could not harm them without harming herself. Something must have gone wrong. She saw the scenario faintly sketched in. The four of them were very close friends and had few outside social contacts (she dismissed Rotary, the Masons and Chapel). They had conceived some scheme or plot – what, Annie could not imagine. Life assurance possibly. She would check up on that angle. In execution of stage one of the plot the three of them had gone off and Agnes had sat there, in Consett, waiting for the stage two call which never came. It would only dawn on her gradually and slowly that something had gone wrong. Annie could imagine her growing embitterment.

What the conspiracy could have been, Annie could not figure out. Whatever it was, however, it posed yet more questions. Little more than an hour ago, Annie had been congratulating herself on extracting from Agnes the "admission" that she had not signed the transfers. But if she was a party to a conspiracy of the four, why on earth should she not sign them. It seemed ridiculous that they should resort to a forgery and incur the risk of prosecution when they could have carried out that part of the scheme with impunity. (Though, thought Annie, was it a forgery if the victims consented – that was one for the lawyers.)

More important, what did all this say about the death on the Ben. Had it been part of the Conspiracy, obviously not a part to which all four subscribed. Or was it that conspiracy going horribly wrong? The latter thesis would go a long way to explaining what had happened subsequently. One thing was clear. As she peeled more and more layers off the truth about the Consett four, it became more and more likely that the unidentified corpse was one of them. And that could only be Edward for it was definitely neither of the women and extremely improbable that it was Arthur, although goodness knows where he was.

Annie had intended to return to the bank to check up on a number of matters. That visit was now much more pressing.

CHAPTER 12

Geoffrey Headley, the bank's assistant manager at head office with whom Annie had dealt was in London on business on the Monday and was not expected to return North until late that evening. She reckoned, however, that it would take little ingenuity to fill in the day usefully. She had concluded that whilst she might be able to believe some things that Agnes had said she hadn't a clue as to which things and intended to check up on as much as she could. If that left her with time in hand and allowed her to slip into Newcastle, do the shops and perhaps go to the cinema all well and good.

It was rather optimistic to expect neighbours to remember with certainty the insignificant events of fifteen months ago so Annie expected to get little. She gleaned only that nobody recalled having seen Agnes for some days after the event (though even these memories were retrospective because it had only percolated through later that there had been an event of any sort). That could mean that she was not to be seen or, alternatively, that she was seen but not remembered. The milkman did not remember either but he was able to recover a tattered order book from the recesses of a cupboard and verify that he had delivered no milk to the Welsby house on the three relevant days in October 1983. As far as he could recall, he had observed his usual practice of not delivering the next day's milk when the previous day's had not been taken in. It sometimes got him into trouble but it usually suited his customers.

So, concluded Annie, Agnes had not even poked her head out of the door to take in the milk. Perfectly possible. No

- this was not quite accurate. Agnes had poked her head out of the door – once. She had said, had she not, that on the day after Arthur left, she had gone round to the Jenkinsons to see Edward, but he had been out and she had returned; if, that is, she was to be believed. If she could, and Annie had enormous reservations about this, then it was odd but far from incredible that she should have returned without bringing in the milk.

Nothing much one way or the other, thought Annie.

One final possibility; she had better exhaust it. Did any of the Jenkinsons' neighbours remember Agnes calling round, as she had said? It was extremely unlikely that they would recall such but Agnes was entitled to the benefit of any corroboration of her story, which might conceivably be forthcoming. She resolved that she would clear this up last thing before she set off back North next day and headed off to spend money in Newcastle.

Geoffrey Headley ushered her into his office the following morning at 10 a.m. sharp and offered her a cup of coffee from an extremely filthy machine on the windowsill. She politely declined and mustered her queries.

First, she wanted to get at the truth of the matter so far as the Welsby transfers were concerned. Had Agnes signed them, despite what she had apparently admitted under the pressure of Annie's interrogation or had her signature been forged? And if the latter, was it possible to ascertain whether Arthur, or Rosemary or anyone else had forged it?

Secondly and more important, had it been Edward's signature on the cheques which had been drawn on the Jenkinson account during the weeks following his disappearance? If not, whose was it? These questions were vital to her investigation and if she could obtain the convenient answers to them her job (although not necessarily that of the Consett force) would be almost done. All the evidence pointed to the body being Edward Jenkinson's except for the cheques. If he had not signed them there was no longer any evidence that he had survived the events, whatever they were, of that day in October 1983. Furthermore, if she could find out who had signed them she had to be well on the way to an explanation of what had happened.

She had not expected answers that day. Headley would have some searching to do to get hold of cancelled cheques and share transfers. She was in the event quite flattened by Headley's first contribution to her endeavours:

"Sorry, can't help you with the cheques. We've no use for them once we've executed the transactions. We hang onto them for a while in case the customer asks for them then we destroy them otherwise we'd be crowded out floor to ceiling by them. We had no reason not to follow our normal practice in Mr. Jenkinson's case. All I can tell you is that since we honoured them we must have been satisfied with the signatures. I'm not saying that they would be subjected to intense scrutiny; we had no reason to suspect anything phoney. But some of them were for largish amounts and we wouldn't just honour them blind."

"And the share transfers," Annie had asked, fearful of the worst there also.

"Can't help you there either, I'm afraid. We handled all Mr. Welsby's business of course but the transfers would be sent on to the relevant company registries and trust offices, etc. They might well have them. You could try."

So except for a list of the registered offices of the

companies and trusts in question Annie appeared to have drawn a complete blank. It began to look like another very largely wasted journey. AND she had wasted two days of her annual leave when Headley suddenly asked her:

"Look, you're only inquiring into an unexplained death, aren't you? Is there any reason to suppose that Mr. Jenkinson was guilty of a serious crime or anything like that?"

"It's perfectly possible," speculated Annie, bearing in mind as she said it that the conspiracy theory was little more than a construct of her own imagination.

Headley was not so easily deceived. "Possible, maybe, but are you able to state on hard evidence that it is probable?"

And Annie had had to admit that she could not – but why had he asked?

"Look, I'm in somewhat difficult position here, confidentiality of clients' business and all that. But I can tell you this. If you think the chap you're trying to identify is Edward Jenkinson, you're barking up the wrong tree."

"How do you know that, Mr. Headley. How can you say that?"

"I can't tell you that. You know that. All I can tell you is that I have every reason to believe that Edward Jenkinson is still our client and that we are still transacting business on his behalf."

"And that's all you can tell me?"

"I'm afraid so. As I say, if he were alleged, on substantial grounds to be guilty of a serious crime I would gladly tell you more, but without that, I can't."

Annie was wondering how to vary her attack so as to worry more information out of him but he came to her rescue:

"Look, I'll tell you what I will do. I'll make my own enquiries, check on what I've told you and if by any chance it turns out that I've misled you, then I'd have to correct that, wouldn't I?"

Annie realized that was the most she was going to get. Her nets were not completely in, however. She still had to go through the formality of interviewing the Welsbys' and Jenkinsons' neighbours about the events of fifteen months previously.

The very first cast brought in a medium-sized fish. The elderly female occupant of the half of the substantial block of semi-detached housing other than that occupied by the Jenkinsons had found the events of the day in question sufficiently memorable. Arthur Welsby had called round. It would be about teatime. They had been waiting for him because he didn't get out of the car and ring the bell or anything. Mrs. Jenkinson had emerged carrying a couple of suitcases, got in the car and they had driven off. Not more than ten or fifteen minutes later, Agnes Welsby had walked round, rung the bell and gone in. This was all she had seen though Mrs. Welsby had not emerged at least for half an hour. All a bit odd, she had thought though not all that much out of character. They were a funny lot, the Welsbys and the Jenkinsons and nothing would really surprise her.

She had heard the Jenkinson's car drive off shortly after that. She didn't know who was in it. It was not for her to pry (i.e. thought Annie, she peered through the curtains too late). What happened after that she didn't know because her son-in-law had called that evening to take her to his place for a few days.

"Was that the last you saw of them? Asked Annie.

The woman paused. "Yes, the last I actually saw of them, the Jenkinsons that is. The Welsbys came back, though. I saw their car outside when Alan, that's my son-in-law, brought me back."

Annie wanted to be clear on one thing. "You say that Agnes Welsby walked round to the Jenkinsons ten or fifteen minutes after Mrs. Jenkinson had left with Mr. Welsby. On the same day, that is. Are you absolutely sure about that?"

"I told you. I left the same evening to go to Alan's for a few days. It stuck in my mind because when Mrs. Jenkinson walked out with her suitcases I was packing mine. There's no doubt about it."

Annie had actually set off back to Fort William. She had thought about the A68 through Otterburn and over Carter Bar but had finally settled for the Tyne Gap. She headed west until she came to the Hexham roundabout, went right round it and headed back to Consett. Her first stop was at a 'phone box from which she rang the Super to make sure that an additional day's leave was in order then she went back to Agnes Welsby's.

CHAPTER 13

Agnes Welsby was not drunk. She was not an alcoholic. She was much too ruthless and integrated for either. But by the time Annie returned, determined to get some sense and, if possible, truth out of her, Agnes was distinctly truculent. More important, she was markedly less perceptive and agile than when Annie had seen her earlier in the day.

At their first meeting, Annie had been altogether too soft. Pity was an emotion best left behind in the locker room. Even courtesy was a mistake more often than not and Annie regretted having given Agnes notice of her first visit. Agnes had had time to get her act sorted out. She had, of course, had the fifteen months to do this but Annie's call had nevertheless given her the chance to make her choices and "psych" herself up for the encounter. Well though she may have learned her part she might well have needed that five minutes by herself in the dressing room before she went on.

Annie had caught her out in one lie. One way or another, Agnes's varied statements as to who had signed the transfers had contained an untruth – a deliberate untruth, furthermore. And Agnes's explanation had also been calculated to deceive; Annie was sure of that. It now looked as though Annie had caught her out in another lie. The neighbour's evidence about the comings and goings at the Jenkinson house on the first day seemed cogent and compelling. Agnes must have put her hat and coat on and headed round to the Jenkinsons pretty well as soon as Arthur had uttered his brusque statement putting an end to the decades of their married life.

That was something else that didn't ring true. When she thought about it Annie could hardly credit that she had accepted Agnes's account of Arthur's departure without question. When your partner of nearly forty years suddenly tells you "I'm leaving you," the one thing you don't do is nothing. You might fly into a rage, set about him with an umbrella, collapse in tears and screams. But from her initial account, Agnes might as well have said, "Very well dear; have you got a clean handkerchief?" Since she did not claim to have produced any of the responses that might have been expected it began to look as though Arthur's announcement had not been "sudden" so far as Agnes was concerned. Had she expected it? Had it, Annie now wondered, happened at all? Or had the conspirators concocted the whole thing, if, that is, it was a conspiracy. It still existed only in her mind and even there an understanding of its nature still escaped her.

Annie decided to tackle Agnes on this first.

"Mrs. Welsby, I would like you to tell me again, if you would, exactly what happened on the day your husband left, when he came home and left, that is."

"I've already told you once, Inspector," grudged Agnes. "Why do you want me to tell you again? Why should I tell you again? You'd think it was me who'd run off with another man." Annie had expected as much. "You told me, Mrs. Welsby, that he came home from work and went straight upstairs. Is that right?"

"I told you."

"You didn't speak. You didn't follow him upstairs or anything?"

"No. Why should I? I'd put the kettle on as soon as I

heard him. I was going to make a cup of tea. I assumed he'd gone upstairs to the toilet and that he'd be down in a minute. Why should I think otherwise?"

"Mrs. Welsby, were you on good terms with your husband?"

"What do you mean? We weren't on bad terms, if that's what you mean. We weren't exactly gooey-eyed either if that's what you want to know. We'd been married over thirty years Inspector and when you've been married that long you don't say a lot and you don't necessarily want to see a lot of each other."

"That sounds like something a bit less than faint praise, Mrs. Welsby."

"I rather think, Inspector, you're asking me about things you couldn't hope really to understand. No, we were long past the starry-eyed stage, but we were perfectly amicable, perfectly content."

"You're saying, are you, that it was a placid, stable, steady marriage?"

"How very perceptive of you, Inspector," replied Agnes with a trace of a sneer.

Annie ignored this and continued: "Will you tell me again just what happened; all that happened, when your husband came downstairs carrying… what was he carrying did you say?"

Agnes sighed. No problem here. "He was carrying a suitcase and he had his sac over his shoulder. It was full."

"And he said what? What did you say?"

"He said 'I'm leaving you Agnes' – that's exactly what he said and it's all he said. He just left."

"And you said nothing, did nothing? He announces after thirty years that he's leaving you and you just let him go? No protestation; no questions?"

"Why, what would you expect me to do, Inspector? Grab him by the ankles; or pull out a gun?" Then, as though she had all at once tired of the game of verbal tug-of-war, she poured out "There's such a lot you don't know, don't understand, Inspector. I didn't care whether he stayed or went. He was a dreadful, dull man. I'd had enough before we'd been married six months. You probably still believe in things like love, romance – going off hand-in-hand into the sunset, don't you, Inspector. Well, I don't. Never have. The scales fell off my eyes many, many years ago. You'll no doubt think it is a very callous, perhaps sad, thing to say, but what matters to me, all that matters to me is this house, the things I have here, my comforts. And, most of all, the knowledge that I need never want as long as I live. Right from the earliest days Arthur has never been anything more to me than a provider. Once he retired, he was useless to me. If you'd given me the chance, I'd probably have thrown him out myself."

"But it still doesn't explain why you did and said nothing, Mrs. Welsby. The actual specific event must have taken you by surprise, him suddenly leaving you, like that?"

"No," insisted Agnes, "I expected it."

This caught Annie on the hop. "What do you mean, you expected it?"

Agnes now hesitated but not long enough. "I knew about him and Rosemary, Mrs. Jenkinson."

Until that point, Annie had only thought in terms of the trio of Edward, Rosemary and Arthur, getting up to whatever it was they did get up to and there was something unexpectedly ordinary and therefore slightly perplexing about Agnes's allegation of a wholly commonplace affair between two only of them. Not sure exactly where to go from there, she temporized with "What do you mean?"

Agnes impatiently retorted, "They were having an affair. Had been for some time. I say "affair" but it must have been a thoroughly sordid hole-in-the-corner business. The never went anywhere, never did anything else."

"How can you be sure of all this, Mrs. Welsby?"

"Oh, when I came to look for them, I could see all the signs. But I knew before that. It was Arthur. I saw the smiles, or rather smirks, the footsie at Bridge. I wondered when she took the job. If she'd wanted just a job, she'd have got one long before that, wouldn't she?"

Now, thought Annie. Agnes had lowered her guard and was letting it all come out. "Why did you tell me earlier that it all came as a great shock to you? Why did you tell me earlier that you only went round to the Jenkinson house the next day?"

Agnes hurriedly tried to regroup her defences. "I did. I didn't know what to do. I wanted to see Edward but he wasn't in. I went round the next day."

"You didn't, Mrs. Welsby. You went round straight away; almost as soon as your husband had left. There are witnesses."

Annie told her about the Jenkinsons' neighbour. Agnes tried to insist that she was mistaken, then lapsed into a sullen silence. Annie pressed on.

"You drove off with Edward Jenkinson, didn't you Mrs.

Welsby?" Annie was not certain about this but it seemed worth a stab.

"No, no I didn't. I went straight back home."

"So you did follow your husband round to the Jenkinsons."

At last. "Yes… yes. I suppose I must have done. It's all a bit confused."

"You haven't seemed at all confused in what you've been telling me so far. And you did leave with Edward?"

Silence.

"Mrs. Welsby, I've given you every chance to tell me yourself what happened. I have to tell you now that we know you were not at home for three days after your husband left. (Partly bluff this but Annie now felt confident it would not be called). "I think it's about time you told me exactly what happened." Agnes had told her. Was this the truth at last?

It was true, Agnes said, that she was not surprised to have it confirmed that Arthur was having an affair with Rosemary and intended to leave her. She was nevertheless caught on the hop by the suddenness of his leaving. She had expected him to have to gird up his loins to break the news. She had no doubt that Rosemary would be the moving spirit. Arthur didn't have it in him. Indeed she thought it quite out of character for Arthur's life to have taken the turn it had.

Anyway, there it was. Arthur had said his brief piece and was out of the house and into the car before she had had time to muster her thoughts. As soon as she did, she went straight into the living room, to the bookcase and pulled out Gibbons' "Decline and Fall…" which was her strongbox. She opened it. She inspected it regularly and was at first relieved to see that the fat, buff envelope was still there. Then she opened that and discovered, in place of the share certificates and bonds she had expected a wad of blank paper. She inferred immediately what had happened. The bonds and certificates were worthless in themselves. Arthur would want to sell them to get the cash and in order to do that her signature would have had to be forged.

She had rushed straight round to the Jenkinsons. She had hoped to catch them but they had left.

She discussed it with Edward and they had decided to try to follow them. They had no idea exactly where they had gone but they knew all the old haunts and it was quite likely they would have gone to one of them.

"Where did you try?" asked Annie.

"Oh, we went first to the Dales and spent a day driving round looking for the car. Then we went to the Lakes, Keswick, then Ambleside. It was all pretty hopeless. We gave up and came back."

"A likely tale," thought Annie. This woman wouldn't know the truth if it hit her in the face.

"You didn't go to Scotland then?"

Agnes quickly remembered the evidence which had brought Annie to Consett in the first place. "Yes, didn't I say? We went to Fort William but they weren't there either. It was hopeless, really. We had no idea where they were."

"You seem to have covered an awful lot of ground in three days."

"Yes. We never stopped."

"Really, Mrs. Welsby, you expect me to believe that it had just slipped your mind that you went to Fort William?"

asked a now somewhat exasperated Annie. Why had she omitted to mention Scotland; what was she trying to hide?

"I wish you would stop harassing me, Inspector. I wasn't trying to give you a detailed itinerary; I..."

She was hedging again, thought Annie. "So you found no trace of them then?"

"No."

"Mrs. Welsby, do you expect me to believe that you set off wandering blindly back and forth across Britain with hardly any idea where they were, hoping to find them?"

"Believe it or not, Inspector, that's how it was. It was all a great shock; we weren't thinking straight."

Annie sensed that Agnes had now settled back into a rut of complacent deception. She decided it was time to deliver another punch.

"Mrs. Welsby, why did you do nothing about the forgeries?"

Agnes again hedged and stuttered but she had no answer to that and the rest of it came out.

Edward and Agnes did not know for sure where the other two were headed, that was true. But they had a pretty good idea. Rosemary had left behind a pile of estate agents' bumph about cottages for sale in the Fort William area. This was, presumably, the reject pile. They shot off hoping to catch Arthur and Rosemary on the road but those two had a half an hour's start and Edward and Agnes arrived in Fort William without having seen a trace of them. They were not unduly concerned. It was a small place and, if they were there, it should be a simple matter to track them down the following day. They would have to find a hotel and if Rosemary had anything to do with it would be a good hotel and all they had to do was work down the list. It was late. They decided to find a hotel for themselves. When Edward went up to the reception desk and asked for a double room in a false name Agnes voiced neither surprise nor dissent. Nor had she any fear, certainly not hope, that Edward would construe her silence as tacit consent to a night of sexual gymnastics. Edward was as keen for revenge as she was.

They did not undress. They lay on the bed and talked and dozed intermittently. Murder was never explicitly mentioned. The nearest they got was Edward's expostulation that he could "happily strangle them with my bare hands." A lust for blood came well down the list of priorities. Hate and greed predominated. The hate would not be assuaged by their deaths. Better that their designs be frustrated and that they be made to suffer. And their ill-gotten gains had to be wrested from them. Avaricious though Agnes was she would as soon have thrown their fortune away as allow Rosemary and Edward to enjoy it. So set on retribution was she that if the price of securing it had been to hand over the whole of her wealth to Edward she would probably have paid it. Fortunately the issue did not arise. Edward was well enough off in his own right. They eventually arrived at the most pleasing scenario. Arthur and Rosemary should emerge from a lengthy spell of imprisonment, apart, to live in poverty, whilst Agnes and Edward lived out the rest of their lives in considerable comfort. The latter became the predominant consideration. Provided that Arthur and Rosemary suffered adequately in some other way, imprisonment and poverty were not essential. They did not intend to kill Arthur and Rosemary but nor were they determined officiously to keep them alive.

They were up early, paid their bill and left without breakfast. They had left Consett in great haste and were ill equipped for the frosty, clear morning which greeted them almost freezing between the hotel door and the car. They stopped and bought overcoats, Edward one of those new anoraks which breathe, Agnes a two-toned ski-jacket. They drew a blank at the Hydro Hotel which had been their first choice. Events later proved that they had been right in their speculation but Arthur and Rosemary had already left. They found no joy at their next two ports of call and were on their way to try the Creagh Ddu Country House Hotel off the Spean Bridge road when they spotted Arthur's car in the golf-club car park. Looking across the golf course they spotted two figures on the Allt a'Mhuilinn path just as it started to rise up to the cwm.

"They're off for Tower Ridge," said Agnes with some astonishment. It did indeed seem preposterous that on the first day of seeking to establish themselves in their new life they should embark on such an enterprise. It was a time, surely, for inspecting rose-covered cottages and chinz suites. Nevertheless, there they were. Edward immediately turned the car round and headed off to the start of the normal route to the top. There, he enjoined Agnes to drive back to the golf club car park and wait for him there. He opened the boot of the car and took out the sac that lived there permanently. Agnes heard him scuffling about and a muttered oath. Glancing round to the back of the car, she saw him take off his jacket and pull on a well-worn Guernsey sweater. He then turned to Agnes, pulling on his new anorak, then the sac on his back.

"No bloody boots," he cursed. "See you in the car park," and with that, headed off up the broad highway to the summit plateau.

That was the last Agnes saw of Edward, nor did she see her husband again. If she was to believed that is. She had driven back to the car park and waited. She had waited all day until well after dark. She had not eaten all day and was ravenous and when she could tolerate the gnawing hunger no longer she decided to nip quickly into the town to find something to eat. She decided she had better leave Edward's car there. She had her key to Arthur's Ford and drove off in that. When she returned, well within the hour, she was annoyed with herself and frustrated to see that Edward's car had gone. It had only just left. A couple of golfers loading their gear into a BMW Estate parked nearby had seen the bloke drive off in it. He had obviously just come down off the mountain, dressed in climbing gear and carrying a large sac. They had glared at him. They did not approve of the car park being used by all and sundry. They had got their message across. He had ducked quickly into his car and driven off. Agnes had been unsure what to do. Edward too would be ravenous. He would wonder where she was, then realize that she must be hungry too and had probably walked off in search of food. He would have driven into the town for a meal hoping, no doubt, to find her. She decided that the best thing to do was to wait for him to return. Then she wondered if Arthur and Rosemary had come down too, found their car missing and reported it. No matter! She had something to report too.

Eventually, she fell asleep.

When she awoke in the morning, she had been more

puzzled than ever. Edward had not returned from the town. God knows what had happened. She went into the town to find some breakfast and tidy up; hoping to see him but there was no sign either of him or of the car. Over breakfast, she decided that whatever had happened, the best thing was to head back to Consett and await events.

She decided to pay one last visit to the car park, drive past just to see if there was anything to be seen. There was, but the Spean Bridge Mountain Rescue Land Rover was not what she had expected. She wondered whether or not to stop and eventually did so. Trying to appear merely curious, she had asked them if something was wrong. It turned out that a badly injured woman had been found up the Allt a'Mhuillin and they were off up to bring her down. No, they did not know who she was; she was "elderly", that was all they knew.

Agnes knew more but did not tell them. It was almost certainly Rosemary.

"Well", thought Annie, the truth at last! Agnes Welsby's account was detailed and convincing. A 'phone call to a colleague on the Spean Bridge Mountain Rescue team reminded her of the fact which she had inexplicably forgotten, that is that there had been a rescue of a woman seriously injured on the Ben at about that time. She excused herself; the Mountain Rescue team was constantly busy and it was easy to forget one incident, especially one in which she had not been personally involved.

She had only one reservation. Could one accept as true an account of events provided by such a habitual liar as Agnes Welsby?

CHAPTER 14

Annie could have kicked herself. Admittedly, you got casehardened to bringing broken bodies down off the mountains and having them carted off to hospital. And there was, experience had taught her, nothing at all unusual about middle-aged women coming to grief in some degree or another. A lot of guff was talked about being properly equipped and keeping away from difficult country but it was true that at least you should be properly shod. It was so easy for even a strained ligament to immobilize a lone walker and in winter that could easily turn to tragedy. Mountain walking was one of the most popular pastimes in Britain and the millions who engaged in it must include some tens or even hundreds of thousands of middle-aged women such as Rosemary Jenkinson. On any given day, thousands of them would be technically at risk and dozens could get into some sort of trouble just as much as any other group.

Nor was there anything particularly surprising about finding such a woman under the north face of Ben Nevis. It was a constant surprise to Annie how many walkers seemed to assume that there was no dangerous terrain in the British hills. Presumably nobody ever succeeded in disabusing them of the belief that all the mountains of Britain were gentle rounded hills with the occasional easily avoided crag. Times without number she had encountered parties of walkers in the Allt a'Mhuillin looking for the way up Ben Nevis, refusing to believe the evidence of their eyes that there was no way up that gigantic cliff that wasn't at least a demanding scramble. It was not peculiar to Britain, she remembered. On a day in the

Aiguilles Rouge when Mont Blanc was out of condition she had been on her way up to the Col du Belvedere for the Aiguille du Lac Blanc when a grey-haired little Welshman had approached her wearing basketball shoes and asked her if that was the way to the Refuge de Pierre a Berard. It was, if you were accustomed to solo descents of 3000 feet of near vertical ice and rock without rope, axe, boots or crampons. They were always lifting walkers off that side of the Ben. More than once some of the few who succeeded in making the ascent from that side had expressed their view to her, in complaining tones, that that side of the mountain was too hard and dangerous for walkers. Apparently she was expected to do something about that but she had never figured out what.

Nevertheless, she could not easily forgive herself for failing to connect the poor wretch they had carried down fifteen months ago with the incident in Glover's Chimney that was now preoccupying her. She had only recently established that the dates coincided and she had it firmly in her mind that Rosemary was now shacked up with Arthur sunning herself on the patio of some Mediterranean villa. She nevertheless angrily hammered her fist into her thigh.

Never mind. Better late than never. It ought to be easy to track the woman down and find out whether or not it was Rosemary although she had almost convinced herself that it was her. And once she had done this she ought to be able to fill the remaining gaps in the mystery and wrap up the whole business fairly quickly. She would greatly welcome this. What had originally been an intriguing problem had now become a compelling pain-in-the-arse and the sooner she closed the file the better.

It turned out to be a simple matter to track down the woman who had been recovered from Tower Gully. They had taken her first to the local hospital which had administered emergency treatment. She had been in terrible shape. She had a complex fracture of the left ankle and one of the right pelvis. One arm was broken and the shoulder of the other one dislocated. And she had a fractured skull as well, obviously, as extensive bruising and abrasions. She had not merely slipped down some scree. She had taken a God-Almighty plunge off somewhere and had fallen a long, long way. By rights she should have been dead.

She had been unconscious when they found her and had remained so on the way to and throughout her stay in the local hospital. She was, in fact, in a coma and as soon as it had been safe enough to transfer her she had been shipped off to Glasgow, to the RVH where they had the expertise and facilities to handle that sort of thing. The Spean Bridge rescue had heard nothing of her since. That was not unusual. Most people they brought down were grateful and many felt that the least they could do was to make a substantial contribution to the Rescue which had no access to public funding. There were still some, however, who thought it was all part of the service and couldn't be bothered even to summons a "thank you". If Annie had thought about it, and she had not, she would just have assumed it was one of those.

Back in Fort William, Annie now rang the RVH for details of the movements of the possible Rosemary. Some revision of the amorous plans would obviously have had to be undertaken as a result of the fall. A lot remained to be explained. She was now almost convinced that it was Edward

Jenkinson who had come to grief on Tower Ridge though she was still mystified as to exactly how it could have happened. It could hardly have been a part of any plan for Rosemary to take such a terrible fall but whatever had happened and however it had happened it had been enough for Arthur to make himself scarce. Annie was far from certain how but it was very likely he who had driven off from the Golf Club car park in the Jenkinsons' car, assuming he had either a key or the technical know-how to manage without one. Rosemary might well have had a key to their car and Arthur would have had access to it; that would likely be the answer to that one.

Rosemary had lain low as well. At least, she had not gone back to Consett. The obvious explanation was that she had somehow contrived to rendezvous with Arthur and resume the interrupted romance. It was a surprise to Annie to discover, when she rang the RVH hoping to find a lead to Rosemary's whereabouts that the poor woman they had brought down that day was still there, in the hospital.

This is where Alan did his bit. Rosemary had remained in a coma for several weeks and they had begun to think that she was unlikely ever to come out of it. She had eventually done so and gradually recovered from her physical injuries but they had turned out to be the least of her medical problems. The experience appeared, hardly surprisingly, to have been utterly traumatic. The amnesia was total and seemed to be complicated by hysteria. The amnesia indeed was probably a manifestation of the hysteria. Although she had recovered consciousness, Rosemary had spoken not a word to any of the hospital staff since. It was not quite true that she had never uttered a sound for she occasionally suffered from convulsions screaming in apparent terror at something. Annie had not found it easy to follow all this over the 'phone and when she had asked for a prognosis it had become more complicated still.

The causes of Rosemary's condition were speculative. The fall itself might induce such a state but if it had been the cause they would have expected some progress before now. The probable explanation was that the hysteria had been induced by something fearfully threatening or terrifying other than the fall and unless they could get at that they could see no way to advance a recovery. It would not have been so bad if the amnesia had not been retrograde i.e. if the trauma had only wiped out her memory of events subsequent to the fall. But the patient gave no indication whatever of any recollection of events leading up to it and without that they could not see how even to start on tackling the problem.

Annie told me all this the night we meet at the Claddach. I immediately suggested:

"Why don't you let Alan have a go at it. It's almost up his street and he's certain to know the people in Glasgow. If you can fill him in on your side of the story he'd be just the man to put it together. I'm sure they'd welcome your help and his."

Annie leapt at the offer and Alan, as I had supposed, was only too willing to offer all the help he could. In fact, it turned out to be very convenient. He was due to spend the following weekend in Glasgow and was on social terms with the consultant in charge of Rosemary's case. Together they made some progress. It was slow though it was not steady. But they managed, enduring a series of crises and setbacks to put Rosemary back together again.

It WAS Rosemary. They had first to be certain of her

identity and, there being no knowledge of the whereabouts of her husband since the day of her fall, it fell to Agnes, her name supplied by the Consett police, to perform this task in the absence of any better witness. Thereafter, Agnes, surprisingly in view of their recent history, visited regularly, if infrequently in the hope of some improvement in Rosemary's condition. On these visits, she would talk to Rosemary and seek to keep her abreast of events but there was no reason to suppose that any such information would reach the understanding of a damaged and amnesiac person.

Establishing Rosemary's identity was the most important weapon they had in the long war to restore her to normality. By recalling her past in Consett, reminding her of places she knew and the life she had led, they gradually bought her to a recollection of her identity. And they finally, shortly after one of Agnes's visits as it happened, made inroads into the amnesia, at least to the extent that it was retrospective. Alan was therefore able to pass onto Annie Rosemary's detailed account of what had happened on that fateful day, right up to the very moment before the assumed traumatic event, whatever it had been. There, Rosemary' recollection of events came to an abrupt end.

Rosemary told them that she had thought right up until the last moment when Arthur drove round to collect her that there was a good chance he would not go through with it. The die was, however, cast. They had cheated Agnes out of her fortune and Agnes was not the forgiving sort, so that she was not surprised when things actually did go according to plan. Rosemary was, she said, elated. A new life full of novel interest if not excitement beckoned. The empty, pointless waste of the past thirty years was to be left behind her. They would become members, if not of the jet set, at least of the Darby and Joan section of it – winters in their Mediterranean villa, summers based in Scotland with trips to wherever in the world they fancied in between; within not too demanding limits, that is.

Rosemary had been somewhat surprised at Arthur's insistence that they should go to Scotland first, but it made sense, even though winter was approaching, to establish their British base first before gadding off to Europe. She had obtained details of everything on the market in the Glencoe/Fort William area, sent to the bank of course, and they had selected six places within the price limits they had set themselves two of which seemed nearly perfect. Rosemary indeed could already imagine herself by the open log fire in the rose-covered stone gatehouse lodge put on the market by an estate on the shores of Loch Leven. To gratify Rosemary they had driven in that way just to try to take a look at it albeit only by moonlight, booking a room by 'phone at the Hydro on the way. She had been delighted with the lodge but Arthur had for some reason taken dead against it and they had almost had a quarrel over trying to extract reasons for his lack of enthusiasm. He had been quite sullen and had hardly spoken over dinner. She knew, however, how to restore his good spirits. She had set about it surreptitiously under the starched white linen tablecloth to such effect that Arthur abandoned his pudding and coffee and they had retired to their room earlier than anticipated.

Rosemary thought that she had earned Arthur's concurrence in a closer look at the gatehouse lodge next day but to her chagrin he was still not reconciled to it. What she dimly appreciated was that he was unlikely to want to look at anything; it was a commitment too far. Oddly, this did not bother her unduly.

He had made it clear that rather than view properties he wanted to climb Tower Ridge of all things. It had been on the agenda. The nearest Arthur had come to enthusiasm about their flight was when he thought about such possibilities. When he had originally suggested it she had accepted the idea but on the assumption that it would feature a long way down the agenda long after they had dealt with the question of finding somewhere to live. She now thought it prudent to put him in a better frame of mind by agreeing to "knock it off." In his present mood there was a risk of him saying "no" once and all to the lodge on which she had set her heart. If she granted his wish today, he would feel obliged to grant hers tomorrow. So they had an early breakfast and set off for the Allt a'Mhuillin stopping at a baker's on the way to pick up an emergency lunch.

They parked at the golf club and set off up. They were in no hurry and took about two and a half hours to reach the Hut. They pressed straight on up and stopped for a rest and a very mean snack at the foot of the gully leading up to the Douglas Gap. They geared up at the bottom. Arthur had insisted that they would need the rope later so they might as well rope up then. He had led off. They had moved together as far as the Gap, then pitched up the chimney onto the ridge proper. It was not a bad day. She was glad they had come; she was enjoying it though Arthur was in an odd mood, excited without being elated was the best way she could describe it to herself.

All went well as they moved together over the Little Tower. Arthur had insisted that they pitch up the Eastern Traverse of the Great Tower but it was not necessary provided that you did not mind pressing yourself against the ice that nearly choked the niche. Then they had got to the crest leading to the Tower Gap. Arthur went slowly but easily along and belayed them at the far end. Then he brought her along. Rosemary had then been astonished to hear Arthur ask her if she would like to lead across the Gap. Certainly not, she had said but he hadn't accepted that. He had claimed to be feeling a bit unwell and said it would be better if she went first and led him across. They were locked in their questionable debate when they were distracted by the sound of scree being disturbed on the far side of the Gap. Looking up they had seen a figure in grey pinstriped trousers scuffed black leather shoes and a new anorak.

There, staring at them from the far side of the Gap stood Edward.

CHAPTER 15

There at the Gap, face-to-face with Edward, Rosemary's recollection of events failed. Annie was bitterly frustrated by it and was ready to believe that some malign influence was governing, if not her life, at least her job. Alan and I urged her not to despair. There was every chance that Rosemary's recovery would continue. She was now at the point of having to confront and learn to live with whatever it was that had provoked the extreme hysteria. No one could be certain that she would ever make the adjustment and take that step. The human mind was a complex and mysterious mechanism. The prognosis was now, however, good, Alan assured her and Annie should not abandon hope of help from that source yet.

All very well, thought Annie, but unless and until Rosemary's memory was further restored where stood her investigation into the identity of the body found in Glover's Chimney? Her instinct told her that it must be Edward Jenkinson but for a number of reasons she could not allow herself to accept this conclusion. There were compelling doubts about it. Applying a familiar criterion she had to admit to herself that they were reasonable and serious doubts.

There was, first of all, the tantalizing information given her by the bank. They claimed still to be doing business with Jenkinson – or was that what they had said? At all events Headley had intended to convey to her his belief that Edward was not dead. He had undertaken to carry out inquiries and contact her if, that belief turned out not to be well founded and he had not come back to her. Ergo, someone who should know apparently still had good reason to believe in Edward's survival and Geordie bank managers were canny souls.

Secondly, why assume, in spite of all she knew about the strange lives of the Consett four, that the confrontation at Tower Gap which Rosemary had described should result in Edward plunging to his death down Glover's Chimney. She made herself imagine what would be the likely consequences of such a confrontation if she had not had the foreknowledge of the corpse in the Chimney. She was obliged to conclude that it would be unlikely to result in the death of one of the three. Rosemary, it seemed clear, had definitely fallen a long way but there was no evidence that that fall had started at the Gap. All that Annie knew was that it had happened after they had reached the Gap and that was not at all the same thing. Anyway, the fact that the confrontation at the Gap had resulted in one extraordinary event (if that indeed were the case) was logically no reason for assuming a second such event.

Then there were all the other possibilities. She reminded herself that she had still not ruled out Sandy Piper though she derived some comfort from the fact that there was no evidence that he had been near the Ben that day. Gerrard did now seem out of the picture. Don Henshaw had seemed to be a thoroughly straight, reliable witness and he was in no doubt that he had seen Gerrard in the Himalayas. Annie, however, now found herself wondering if Don could possibly have confused that trip with a previous expedition or if it might not have been a case of mistaken identity. "Gerrard" she remembered had not acknowledged Don. Don had assumed that he was standoffish. Might it not be, though, that "Gerrard", not being Gerrard and not knowing Don had simply not realized that he was being addressed?

118

Annie remarked to herself that she had many times previously had to remind herself that if you cared to question it there was almost no proposition that you were incapable of doubting.

Then there were Kendall and McNee. Tom's evidence surely made them both very serious contenders, especially Kendall. Come to think of it, if she had to choose between Kendall and Jenkinson, which did she think more likely?

That was when the internal phone buzzed. It was the desk sergeant.

"Yes, what is it?"

"There's a gentleman here would like to speak to the person in charge of the investigation into the body they brought down off the mountain ma'am."

Puzzled, Annie had thought for a moment but there was nothing else that was urgent or pressing. "Oh, show him in," she said, quickly adding after the shortest of pauses "Who is it?"

"It's a Mr. Andrew McNee," replied the sergeant.

How much publicity attends a death in the mountains varies according to the circumstances. It is a bit like dogs biting children. It happens all the time and isn't worth a line of print by itself. About every five years or so, a Rottweiler kills a baby and that, understandably, makes the headlines. When it does you can bet that there will be an epidemic of "dog savages child" stories in the papers during the ensuing weeks.

It's much the same with death in the mountains. An isolated death may merit a column-inch on page six of the national dailies. A second one hot on the heels will get rather more coverage. And if there is a third, "investigative journalists", i.e. the ones who always assume that somebody is to blame for something and bitch about it, will get their teeth into it. Climbers are idiots; kids are badly-trained, interviews with rescue-leaders, pressed to distribute blame, will usually, frustratingly, reveal them to be normal people, their sometimes extraordinary courage not at all obvious.

The discovery in Glover's Chimney had excited rather more interest than is usual. It was, it is true, an isolated death but the fact that the body had been headless had been there for some time and was unidentified made it worth four to six column inches on the bottom half of page 2. Annie had had a stream of 'phone calls from the press during the days following the discovery but there had been no further news and interest had waned. At first, there was a honeymoon period during which only identification would be news and, there being none, the national dailies had forgotten all about it. There then came a point, however, at which the fact that the body had still not been identified prompted an interest of a different kind to those, at least, who still remembered the incident. In this case, a local reporter had troubled to mention that it was still not known who it was and the national papers had picked it up. The thrust had switched from tragedy to mystery.

Andrew McNee had been stunned when he read the initial report of the finding of the corpse in his "Mirror". He had been sure that Gerry would come to harm given the predicament he had left him in. For several days after his impetuous departure from Fort William fifteen months previously he had searched the papers for news of Gerry. He had sped off south getting away from the area as fast as he could and it was only when he got beyond Carlisle and onto a stretch of the M6 that he called "home" that he was able to relax a little and sort himself out. He could not go back to his old haunts in Manchester and Macclesfield. They would catch up with him there. He would have to drop out, not just for a while but forever. He would have to start a new life.

A train robber would have gone to Brazil or at least the Costa del Crime. A spy would end up in Moscow. The horizons of the working classes in Lancashire are not, however, so broad and McNee had ended up in Preston for no better reason than that it was at about that point on the journey that he came to reconcile himself to his conclusion. It had turned out to be a far more intelligent choice than either Brazil or the Costa del Crime for he had been totally inconspicuous. He spoke the language; the town was large enough for everybody to be a stranger. Although the news had not, apparently, reached Whitehall vast numbers of unemployed in South Lancashire had got on their bikes and gone out looking for work. It had been an easy task for McNee to find lodgings and pass himself off as an itinerant Merseysider in search of work.

And had found it easy to get work. His years as a self-employed painter and decorator had taught him how. Too often he had tendered for jobs only to find himself undercut by cowboys whose costings did not include PAYE and VAT. Even where he was not competing for work he had occasionally quoted a price only to be asked, with a hint of a wink "How much off for cash?" In the *haut monde* of "interior design" in Prestbury the payment of taxes had seemed to be unknown. It was simply assumed that VAT would not be charged and, if it was, you got no more work. He was good at his job and it had simply been a matter of going through the Yellow Pages until he landed a job, "self-employed" of course, and no questions asked. This suited McNee down to the ground. He wanted to lay no trace via the social security system.

After eight months in and outs of "black work" he had gone into business on his own account, left his digs and rented a flat. He had found friends of his own sort and gradually came to feel secure. He was used to immersion in an unusual sub-culture and probably adjusted more readily to being "on the run" than would most. He had therefore been stunned to read, in the Lancashire Evening News bought on the way home one evening that an unidentified corpse had been recovered on Ben Nevis.

The two weeks that followed broke hm. They were more than he could take. There was no compelling reason whatever to assume, after all this time, that it was Gerry. Yet the reports said that the body had been there for a long time and that it had been recovered from the "Towering Ridge" area of the mountain. What he could not understand and what really screwed him up was how it had taken all this time for the news of his fall to break. He would have gone after Gerry himself at the time if only he hadn't been sure the others would see to him. He still could not understand how they had missed him and how his body had remained undiscovered all this time.

He had been tempted to rush off straight away to try to find out and put his mind at rest but he had disciplined himself to wait. They would identify the body – find out who it was. It couldn't be Gerry; he must be alright. If by some chance (which McNee could not explain) it was Gerry he would have to be able to think calmly about what to do. So he had forced himself to sit tight and await events.

Only they had not evened. Each day for a fortnight he had bought all the papers and poured over every inch of them. He had even gone out of his way, down to the station, to buy The Scotsman but not a word. Eventually it had become too much. He had decided he must get up to Fort William and find out what he could and that had been his intention as he boarded the train. But during the long hours of the journey he had changed this resolve. Over the intervening fifteen months he had gradually come through the initial phase of fear and guilt and, bit-by-bit, allowed himself to believe that it was something in his past; that he had an open future free from retribution in a second life unconnected with the first. This triumph of self-deception had been brutally wrested from him and it was much worse now than it had ever been during the days immediately after it had happened.

Had there not been a chink of doubt about his guilt – a possibility that what he had done was excusable even if reprehensible – it is doubtful if he would have gone to the police that day. He was no lawyer and was thus in no position to make a refined judgment about the legal consequences of what he had done. But he knew in his own mind that it was not murder. He had not meant Gerry to die. Anyway, whatever the consequences it was better off his chest. He would pay whatever penalty the law exacted, however long it took, and then become a free man again. There was no other way he would ever be able to claim his freedom.

Annie had been taken by surprise by the desk sergeant's call and had had no more than a few moments to prepare herself for her visitor.

As he walked through the door Annie saw immediately that the description she had had of McNee had been a fair one. He was wearing a rather soiled old down jacket which, she noted, had endured some rough passages. There were traces of paint on his well-worn brogue shoes and she imagined that his creaseless grey flannel trousers had done service for a considerable length of time. She ushered him into a chair. She had not had time to order her thoughts and anyway he had asked to see her. "Let him make the running," she thought. "I'll play it by ear." Hot on the heels of this thought came another. McNee did not know that she was onto him. He knew nothing about her visits to Manchester and Macclesfield; at least, she had no reason to think he did. As long as she didn't let on she would be well placed to tell whether he was trying to deceive her or not in whatever he had to tell her.

"Good afternoon, Mr. McNee, how can I help you?"

"It's about the body they found on Ben Nevis, by Tower Ridge, miss."

"Yes, what about it?"

"It was in all the papers."

"Yes, I know. What about it Mr. McNee?"

"Well, I wondered if it had been identified yet."

Annie hesitated. "No, well not yet. Not definitely, that is," then, trying to nudge him in the right direction, she added "But we've got a pretty good idea."

They spoke together, her "Why do you ask?" clashing with his "Who do you think it is them?"

She left it to him to take it up. "I think I know who it is."

"Who would that be, Mr. McNee?"

"It's Gerry Kendall, isn't it?"

"It could be, Mr. McNee," (true, it could be but it was another of Annie's "black truths", statements literally true but calculated to mislead.) "But what makes you think it is? Don't you think it would be a good idea if you told me all about it, beginning to end, instead of hedging about like this?"

McNee was just about ready to tell her. It didn't much matter whether it was Gerry any more. If it wasn't, so much the better but either way he wanted the business settled one way or the other.

Annie clinched it. "Look Mr. McNee, we know all about you. We've been looking for you for some time. We know all about you and Gerry Kendall, the business," (She contrived to sound as though he could look forward to several years for fraud and tax-evasion, if nothing else). "We know about the bill you left unpaid at the Fairmont on the morning when you left. You may as well tell me all about it." A pause, then "How about a cup of tea? Let me take your jacket."

Then McNee told her.

He had absolutely insisted that Kendall accompany him that day on the Ben. He had had enough. The time had come to settle things one way or the other. When he and Kendall had first got together he had been "swept off his feet." Annie would find it difficult to understand that but he'd never met anyone like Kendall before. At first they had got on marvellously. Kendall dazzled and at the same time flattered McNee. McNee would never otherwise have agreed to Kendall's hare-brained scheme. He, McNee, had been doing alright on his own. Kendall had turned out to be a total dead weight – full of bright ideas and grandiose schemes but when it came to the crunch, didn't know one end of a paintbrush from the other. He could have tolerated that but it was all take and no give with Kendall He, McNee had been going to the hills since he was a lad. It was about the only part of his life that he positively liked. He had always had the weekends to look forward to; thinking and planning what he might do got him through the week. It would have been terrific if Kendall had come to share his enthusiasm but he never tried, always crying off because of a sprained ankle or a sore toe or something else.

Even that would have been tolerable if Kendall hadn't been so bitchy about him going off without him; started accusing him of having affairs with other men and not wanting Kendall around. Ironic, that. Things had got to the stage where McNee spent all week nursing Kendall through whatever job they were currently engaged in but without the saving grace of a pleasurable weekend to look forward to. Kendall had killed that. He, McNee couldn't go on like that. He hadn't just suggested a few days in Scotland on the spur of the moment. Although Kendall had not known it, it was "make or break" so far as McNee was concerned. It was Kendall's last chance.

But he wouldn't take it. He had refused to go out, feigned a cold or, rather, 'flu – all his colds were 'flu and if he'd had 'flu it would have been double pneumonia. On the last day, McNee absolutely would not take a refusal. They had had a God-Almighty row in their room before breakfast and it had broken out again when they came down to breakfast.

That was what had made McNee decide. They were going out; Kendall was going whether he liked it or not. Either Kendall shaped up or McNee was going to finish with him when they came down.

"As God's my witness, that's all I had in mind when we

set off," swore McNee.

He had decided on Tower Ridge as the test piece. It had taken them nearly three hours to get to the Hut, Kendall stopping every few minutes for a rest, then another forty minutes to get to the foot of the gully leading to the ridge above the Douglas Boulder. Kendall had complained of a migraine all the way. He had twice broken down in tears. When they got to the foot of the gully he just lay down, said he couldn't go a step further and pretended to collapse. That didn't fool McNee; he was determined. He fastened Kendall's harness on him, with no help from Kendall, tied them both on and set off up the gully. He had had to wrench Kendall to his feet with the rope and practically drag him all the way up to the Douglas Gap.

There, they had another bout of sobbing but McNee had set off up the chimney onto the ridge proper. He had had no protection from Kendall – he didn't need it but he thought it spoke volumes for Kendall's attitude that Kendall put his histrionics above his, McNee's, safety. The struggle continued all the way up the easy part of the ridge. Then they had come to the Great Tower. It had taken half an hour of swearing and cajoling to get Kendall through the niche on the Eastern Traverse and when they got to the fine crest that leads to Tower Gap he had had literally to drag Kendall along on his hands and knees. That brought them to the Gap. McNee had made Kendall safe on the crest and had fixed a sling around the block and tied into that. Then he had stepped carefully across and up. He expected no help from Kendall and got none. He tied himself on the far side. Then he had turned to the task of getting Kendall across.

This time, Kendall had to help himself. He had to untie himself and remove the protection on the block. There was no way McNee could physically drag him across. Kendall had absolutely refused entirely ignoring his own predicament. He had groaned and screamed and sobbed.

"We were stuck there, like that, for nearly half an hour," said McNee to Annie. "At first, I was bloody furious – I called him everything under the sun. It was so frustrating; it seemed to say it all. Unless he untied himself there was nothing I could do. The bugger seemed absolutely determined to spoil everything for me. He seemed not to give a damn about me at all." McNee paused. "Then, all of a sudden, I'd had enough. I was sick and tired of carrying him, at work, on the hill, emotionally. He had totally, selfishly, destroyed what could have been a wonderful experience. I decided he was going to have to take responsibility for himself. I'd had enough. He was going to have to look after himself. I wasn't going to look after him any more. I didn't say anything to him. I just started to untie myself. Now he noticed and stopped snivelling." "What are you doing?" he asked. "You can't do that." But I did. I just took off the rope and threw it across the Gap at him. I said something like "look after yourself for a change" or "get yourself off" or something like that and set off up the summit tower on my own."

McNee dried up, took a sip of tea. Annie insisted "but you must have known it was a vicious thing to do, a desperate situation for him. Didn't you think? He'd likely kill himself."

"Oh, I thought alright," McNee had replied. "I didn't just think; I hoped he'd kill himself. It was like leaving it to the fates. I expected him to die and I wanted him to." Then, suddenly, almost inaudible "and he did, didn't he. I thought it would be ideal, solve everything."

McNee had almost shrunk into himself. Annie thought he had finished but pressed him a bit further. There was something she still wanted sorting out.

"You saw him fall did you, Mr. McNee?"

"Yes," whispered McNee. "I saw him go."

"You just left him, you knew he couldn't look after himself." The mountaineer was taking over from the policewoman and she was angry. "You did nothing about it. You may say you love the hills, Mr. McNee but you don't belong there."

"No, no," McNee corrected. I would have helped him but I thought the others would see to him. I still can't understand why they didn't, how they can have missed him."

"What do you mean, what others?" Annie was puzzled.

"I was going to go down to him but there were two others, one going down the gully, one at the bottom, coming up. I was sure they'd seen him go; sure they were going to help. I was going to go down the gully myself but I thought 'what good would it do?' I'd have had to explain. There was the business of me having untied, etc. I didn't know what to do for the best. I felt so bad about it. I decided eventually to look after number one. I headed off down the easy way to Fort William."

"Have you any idea who these two were, Mr. McNee?"

"No, I'm sorry. I haven't. I had a brief word with the one I later saw going down but I didn't know him."

"He was on the ridge at the same time as you, was he?" Annie was trying to get the time-map straight in her mind.

"Not on the ridge, at least not so far as I know. He left

the summit just before I got there and headed off down."

McNee was conning her, Annie suddenly thought. "You'd better think again. You can't see Number Two Gully from the summit side of the ridge; you certainly can't see down Glover's Chimney from there."

"I'm not talking about Number Two Gully." There was a touch of impatience in McNee's voice. "He fell down Tower Gully."

Annie had gone over it again with him. Yes, he knew the Ben fairly well. He certainly knew the difference between Tower Gully and Number Two Gully and it was down the former that Gerry had gone. McNee was in no doubt about that. It would have been, let's see, getting on for an hour after he'd left Gerry at the Gap; perhaps not as long as that. He had continued up to the summit – that would take fifteen or twenty minutes, wouldn't it? He'd sat at the summit for maybe ten or fifteen minutes – smoked a fag. Then he'd set off down. He had intended to descent over Carn Dearg but went to the edge to get a view of the Ridge. That was when he had seen the body bounding down the gully.

He still couldn't believe it. But he understood that he needed to get the Hell out of there as soon as he could.

CHAPTER 16

McNee's "confession" had left Annie with a ragbag full of bits and pieces. At least she could cross Andrew McNee off her list of candidates (assuming the creature now occupying one of the cells downstairs was McNee; there seemed to be little doubt about this but experience had taught her to make the cautious reservation all the same). For the life in her, she couldn't see how Gerry Kendall could remain on the list either. If what McNee said was true – and why on earth should she mistrust a man who had confessed to a very serious crime (as well as the minor one for which he was currently held in custody) – there seemed no possible way Kendall could have ended up in Glover's Chimney. No force of nature could possibly have got him there. A lot of things could have got a body down from there to where Kendall had last been reported – avalanche, frost, rock fall. But not in the reverse direction. Conceivably, he could have got into Glover's Chimney as a result of human agency but how or why baffled her.

Could he somehow have got there under his own steam? It seemed impossible. A fall such as he had undergone must have caused death or at least serious injury and even a minor injury would have been enough to prevent a re-ascent of the Ridge. And, anyway, even if he could have got there, was it credible that Kendall should set out again, alone, up Tower Ridge which he abhorred in order to fall conveniently into Glover's Chimney and solve Annie's problem. Unlikely, she felt.

Not even booking McNee had been simple. He had, she was sure, committed one crime – theft from the Fairmont Hotel. And Annie had eventually decided to charge him with that. It enabled her to shelve for the time being the wholly unprecedented problem of one who had confessed to a serious crime (for had the facts been as McNee supposed it would surely be manslaughter at least) of the actual commission of which there was insufficient evidence. For manslaughter, after all, you needed a death consequential upon the act. Annie remembered the lecturer at police college speculating whether there could be such a thing as attempted manslaughter. He had thought not. Annie wondered what he would make of this.

One had to keep a level head in these matters, difficult though that was in the instant case. Rule One: the obvious and probable explanation was almost invariably the correct explanation. Kendall had taken a bad fall. McNee's assumed rescuers must actually have rescued Kendall. Kendall must have been very fortunate to escape death or even serious injury. But it had not proved necessary to call out the Rescue. They had managed to get him off the mountain without assistance and he had gone his way. It was a very improbable coincidence that he should take such a tumble at about the same time another and unconnected victim was heading down Glover's Chimney but that was the conclusion she was forced to. A coincidence it had to be.

Annie would have felt more assured about these deductions if she had known which way Kendall had gone and, in particular, where he ended up. Well, hospital wasn't a bad start. He could hardly have walked away completely unscathed if McNee's account was at all accurate. Something, surely, would have needed patching up. She resolved to put Dick onto it. The Super could hardly complain. It was now a suspected manslaughter case, wasn't it?

For a couple of days nothing happened. Annie busied herself with the rest of her neglected caseload. Then two argosies arrived bearing modest treasure.

The first was the product of Dick's search of the hospital records for information about Gerry Kendall. Following the line of least resistance he had started with the local hospital and struck it rich immediately. The search had not finished there but they had given him the vital lead. He reported to Annie:

"He must have gone straight there when he got down. They registered him the same day. Apparently he went to outpatients but they needed only a cursory examination to admit him. They kept him there for about five days then transferred him to Edinburgh."

Annie inferred "So he must have been more badly knocked about than they thought, then. It's often that way. No particularly obvious outward and visible signs but serious internal injuries when the experts get at them…"

Dick interrupted: "No, that's the thing. Not a mark on him or in him. No injuries of any sort at all apparently. I assumed the same as you, asked what his injuries were. 'What injuries' they asked. We thought we'd got two different blokes mixed up."

"What then" asked Annie "did he go into hospital for?"

"Turned out he had viral pneumonia."

"Viral pneumonia. Couldn't they cope with that here then?"

"Oh, they could cope with the pneumonia alright, but it turned out he had this AIDS thing."

Annie could not help but register the irony. It was

Kendall who had been so screwed up about McNee's promiscuity but it was Kendall who had fallen victim. "That's why they carted him off to Edinburgh is its? Because of the AIDS?"

"That's right. Actually they say it wasn't AIDS or so the bloke I dealt with confided in hushed tones. According to him AIDS is just a prototype, an inefficient forerunner. Poor Kendall was accorded the privilege of being one of the first to contract some sort of super-AIDS. Apparently, it's only just getting started. We ain't heard nothing yet. Within a generation we'll all be dead."

"You keep your pessimistic prognostications to yourself. How is Kendall?"

"Oh, didn't I tell you? He died shortly after they got him to Edinburgh. He was well on the way when he reported into the local hospital. Must have been a rough time for him for several months before that apparently."

Dick left and Annie sat alone pondering the news. So the poor sod had got off the Ridge by himself, had he? What a very gutsy thing to do. Needs must, she supposed. Anyway, he hadn't fallen. He could not have taken the tumble McNee described and survived it completely unscathed.

Who or what she suddenly wondered had McNee seen? More than that, who were the two mystery men McNee had seen approaching the victim?

There could be only one answer to the first of these questions. It had to be Rosemary. It was true that plenty of people got into difficulties but there was not exactly a constant flow of people peeling off the north face of Ben Nevis in October.

The conclusion that it was Rosemary posed more questions than it answered. Rosemary had been discovered early the following morning by a couple of young Dundee climbers who had gone up to the Hut late the night before. They had set off for North-East Buttress early the following morning and there she was. One had stayed with her and the other had got down in remarkable time to get the Rescue up to her. Where, wondered Annie did this leave the two mystery men? Was it credible that they had got to her but then left her on the mountainside to die? If so, theirs was a reasonable expectation. It was indeed a miracle that she had survived the night. It seemed more likely, as McNee had been forced to speculate, that they had missed her. More likely possibly but still far from probable.

Annie's intellectual gymnastics were interrupted by the 'phone. She welcomed it. She picked up the receiver and announced herself.

"Inspector Chisholm? Hello. This is Headley, manager, Lloyds, Consett."

"Hello, Mr. Headley; nice to hear from you."

"Well I don't know about that, I'm afraid."

"Oh?" she wondered. She wondered whether it would have been nice to hear from him and she wondered if his 'bad' news might be her 'good' news.

"Yes, I did some checking on Edward Jenkinson, as I promised."

"Yes".

"I think I can now tell you this. We received instructions from Mr. Jenkinson to clear his account ever quarter and send the balance to another account."

"Yes Mr. Headley." Why didn't he get on with it?

"The instructions were contained in a type-written letter signed by Mr. Jenkinson. That is to say we thought it was signed by Mr. Jenkinson but it turns out it wasn't. At least, we've had it checked by Forensic Science in Morpeth against his signature on our account documents and according to them it is 'highly probable that the signatures were penned by different hands'. That's what they say."

"Well, that's a turn up for the books" was Annie's appropriate cliché of the day. Her mind was down a siding, studying a sort of coincidence, which would have interested Arthur Koestler. Had Headly not 'phoned and had she been left to pursue her own thoughts she would just about have arrived at the very same conclusion that Headley's news had carried her to and at just about the same point in time. At last she had it. The last obstacle had been removed. The body they had brought down from Glover's Chimney was that of Edward Jenkinson after all. The only reason for not subscribing to that conclusion had at last been removed and her instinct had been vindicated.

Her reverie was interrupted by Headley's voice.

"Hello Inspector Chisholm, are you there?"

"Yes, sorry Mr. Headley; just taking in what you told me. I'm very grateful to you indeed for the trouble you've taken. It makes things a lot clearer." She was signalling, in that barely perceptible way that one does, that she was angling to put the 'phone down.

"Wait a minute, Inspector."

"I'm sorry."

"Don't you want to hear the rest of it?"

The rest of what, Annie pondered.

"Our instructions were to send the balances through to Mr. Jenkinson's account, that is to say what we were told was Mr. Jenkinson's account in Leuven."

"Where?"

"Leuven, Louvain, in Belgium."

"Well, if it wasn't Mr. Jenkinson's account, whose was it?"

"That's the trouble, I'm afraid. They won't tell us. Contrary to their policy they say. I expect you police will have ways of finding out about that sort of thing," Headley chuckled.

"We'll have to see what we can do," Annie stalled.

She took the details from Headley, bank's name, address, account number etc. Her thanks to him were sincere. He had, she reckoned, more or less finally settled the question of the identity of the corpse. His other contribution could not be avoided. It now appeared beyond doubt that Edward Jenkinson's death was inextricably mixed up with serious crime. She need no longer shrink into a corner when she saw the Super approaching.

CHAPTER 17

There had been so many twists and turns in her investigation thus far that Annie's attitude to the whole business had become one of defensive pessimism. The primary function of the discovery that someone was forging Edward Jenkinson's signature, she had to remind herself, was merely to negative the only evidence that he had survived the events of October 1983. That function was discharged; she must expect no more. She could not, however, remove from her mind the fact that the evidence of forgery was significant in at least two other respects.

One of these did not bother her all that much. The forgery was a crime; of that there could be little doubt. It was certainly a forgery by the law of Scotland and England and she would have been astonished to hear that it was a permissible social activity in Belgium. She did not know where the crime had been committed. It was more likely than not that the letter authorizing the transfers had been written abroad. It occurred to Annie that it was possible that the bank in Consett might be able to shed some light on this but a quick 'phone call putting the query to them had soon been returned without taking her any further. The letter bore the Jenkinson's Consett address and none of the secretaries who might have opened it could remember what stamp the envelope in which it came bore. That created a slight presumption that the envelope was unremarkable and had therefore been posted in Britain but no more than that. Even however, if the letter had been written abroad it would not necessarily cease to threaten the Queen's peace she now realized.

It was like shooting somebody across a national frontier. Where was the murder committed? Even if the letter had been posted in Belgium (or France or Switzerland or anywhere else for that matter) its potential for fraud and deceit had been realized in Consett. She experienced a sinking feeling as she groped around the recesses of her mind trying to retrieve what little she had learned at college about the criteria for assumption of jurisdiction by British courts finally saying to herself "What the hell, that's Consett's problem not mine."

The other respect in which the fact of forgery was significant was Annie's problem and it did bother her. Whilst she was satisfied that it was Edward Jenkinson's body which had lain up there on the mountain all that time (well, almost certainly she cautioned herself) she still hadn't a clue how he had come to grief. She tried to apply Rule One. Jenkinson had not had his boots with him. He had gone off up Ben Nevis in a pair of smooth-soled black leather town shoes.

"Christ," she kicked herself. The body was wearing a boot.

Annie almost gave up. "What am I doing here?" she asked herself. She frequently thought the grass looked greener in the other field and the metaphor came into her mind now (with the irritatingly pedantic modification that if you looked at grass closely, it was more yellow than green as every painter knew). She would find it relatively easy to qualify as a mountain guide and in these increasingly feminist days she would have a very good chance of making a fair living out of it. Why put up with this hassle? Every time she encountered a reason for believing that she had solved the puzzle of the body on the Ben, hot on the heels came a reason for doubting her solution.

139

Heaving a sigh, however, put up with it she did.

Stick to Rule One. Edward Jenkinson had not had his boots with him. He had gone off up Ben Nevis in a smooth-soled pair of black leather town shoes. He had not conveniently found a pair of climbing boots by the side of the path as he mounted; he had not stuck to terrain that was relatively safe. Annie had Rosemary's evidence that Edward was still wearing his shoes when he appeared on the other side of the Gap. So, Rule One, anyone who comes to grief on terrain like that whilst wearing smooth-soled shoes probably comes to grief BECAUSE he is wearing a pair of smooth-soled shoes. *Post hoc et propter hoc.* The summit is steep she reminded herself but not so steep as not to hold a lot of loose scree. Furthermore the rock might have been wet. That side of the Ben was covered in drainage. That was one reason why the ice was so good. So far as she knew only Edward Jenkinson had been wearing smooth-soled leather shoes that day. He WAS the likeliest victim, ok?

Annie gripped her mind tight. If it was probable that Edward was the victim at that point in time when he stood across the Gap wearing his shoes that probably was a fact and it could not logically cease to be so as a result of anything that had happened subsequently. Had he, for example, got off the mountain unharmed it would have been nonsense to say to him "Obviously you were perfectly safe and at no risk – you can clearly do it again with impunity." If then one assumed for purposes of argument that what was probable had actually happened, Edward had fallen and the question that had to be answered was "How come, having been wearing shoes, he was found fifteen months later wearing a boot?"

Annie checked the inventory; he had been wearing one

of a standard pair of Galibier boots, a bit old-fashioned but still preferred by many of the "more mature" members of the climbing community who had grown up with them and who did not take kindly to the new-fangled Koflach plastic.

While she had the inventory in front of her she confirmed that the victim had been found wearing the tattered remnants of what seemed at one time to have been a pair of best worsted grey pinstriped trousers. She knew one climber who had been on a celebrated Himalayan expedition in the 1950s who habitually wore a pair of breeches made out of sailcloth during his Navy days. Best wool worsted was as good as most things; better, indeed, than the standard cotton corduroy that was so popular.

It all went to confirm that the body was Edward's. If that was so there was no escaping the conclusion that if he had fallen his footwear had been changed between the moment when Rosemary had observed him standing at the far side of the Gap and the time when he was discovered by Alan and I in Glover's Chimney. She tried to imagine how and why.

She conjured up a, conversation between Arthur and Edward. "I say old chap, bit dicey sporting footwear like that, what? Here, take my boots, old fellow." "Dashed sporting of you, I must say, but do keep them for yourself," etc. That did not seem likely. Then something else came at her from an angle. Why had she been having all this extraordinary difficulty identifying the body? She had never encountered the problem before. At least not on anything like this scale. The reason was clear. There was an almost total lack of identifying features. That was, when she thought about it, very odd. There was always something – driving licence, chequebook, credit card stuck in the top of a sac. Even, she recalled, an old RAF service number black-inked in the corner of an ancient waterproof cape on one occasion. Yet in this case there had been nothing, nothing that is except the sales tag in the new anorak which had led them to Edward in the first place and no one would think of that as a document of identity. She reminded herself that the anorak could have belonged to four or five others, not necessarily Edward.

Annie sidled hesitantly towards the inference that the body had deliberately been cleaned of all identifying features. That might explain the lost sac. For a moment she wondered gruesomely if it might account for the lost head but Dr. Kenny had been clear on how that had happened. It might, however, explain the shoes. She had to know whether it did and she had to know NOW.

It took her several attempts to impress on Jack Birtley in Consett the urgency and importance of her query. At first he had been reluctant to do anything at all and had pooh-poohed the suggestion that such an exotic fact could possibly have any relevance to real police work which was a great impertinence, thought Annie, since he knew practically nothing about what was going on at all. Then he had grudgingly agreed to get someone to look into it when he had time, which Annie suspected, and rightly, was just a paraphrase for saying that he would do nothing. She had had to nag him constantly for ten minutes before he had realized in which direction lay the quiet life and undertaken to make inquiries immediately:

"Yes, yes, alright," he had almost shouted down the 'phone. "I'll check on it now, right away. I'll call you back," nearly deafening Annie with the sound of the receiver being slammed down.

It had imposed an undue strain neither on Birtley's ingenuity nor on Consett's resources. A 'phone call to "Jenkinson & Co" and a chat with Edward's former secretary had established that Edward had been a meticulous, almost fussy, dresser and had always had his shoes made, as had his father before him, by one of Newcastle's few remaining bespoke shoemakers. His shoes always bore not only the shoemaker's own mark but the customer's name. Gratified to hear this, Annie had made a half-hearted attempt to patch things up with Jack Birtley and had joked "I wonder how his secretary comes to have such an intimate knowledge of his clothing habits" to which Birtley had humourlessly replied "nothing unusual about that if you actually knew Edward Jenkinson, that is," adding, after a pause "and Rosemary Jenkinson as well." Annie had left it at that, thanked him and rung off hoping she would have to have no further need to ask a favour of him.

After she put the 'phone down she asked herself out loud "and where does that get us?" Where it got her, she decided, was that the most likely scenario could almost certainly be ruled out. Practically all deaths in the mountains were accidents and that had throughout been the most probable explanation of Edward Jenkinson's death. Certainly some odd things had gone on but they were all consistent with being consequent upon an accident and nothing had affirmatively established that the poor soul in Glover's Chimney had met his end as a result of foul play. That, Annie now had to recognize was no longer probably the case.

An accident might make people do stupid things.

Particularly if the people associated with it were swimming in a sea of guilt they might behave peculiarly, even reprehensibly. Annie had actually had a case in Glencoe where one bastard off on a dirty climbing weekend had abandoned his badly injured fancy woman and 'phoned the Rescue anonymously lest the news of the accident and his involvement in it percolated back to his wife. It had been a miracle that they had found the girl and got her off alive. But this was a different ballgame. Some person (or persons) had set about rendering the about-to-be corpse of Edward Jenkinson unidentifiable. It had been someone, furthermore, who knew that to achieve this objective his shoes would have to be removed. That was most likely to be Rosemary Jenkinson, possibly Arthur Welsby but almost certainly the two in concert. Of all the various possibilities only they would know that. Furthermore, only they would have been threatened by the discovery of Edward's identity. It would lead straight back to them. It would take an investigator nowhere near any of the others who had been on or near the Ridge that day.

But was that the only help that Annie could glean from these deductions? Since Edward's death someone had been impersonating him, at least forging his signature so as to gain access to the funds in his accounts. In order to take that risk, that person (or persons!) would be very likely to know that it was safe and purposeful to do so. They would have to have reason to believe that there was a high degree of probability that no questions would be asked, most particularly by the person whose funds were being rifled. Nothing could make it more probable that Edward Jenkinson would raise no queries than that he was dead. They would have to know, in other words, that he was dead – but they would also have to be able to rely on the fact that no-one else, particularly his bank, would be aware of his death. That pointed unmistakably to Arthur and Rosemary.

It was Arthur who, in the event, had become the sole beneficiary. The "accident" (if that is what it was) to Rosemary had unexpectedly left Arthur with the whole of the profits of the enterprise, whatever it had been, rather than the half-share he had originally expected. Hold on though, there was more than one-way into the Jenkinson treasure chest. Rosemary was Edward's wife. Would it not make a lot more sense looking at it from her point of view for her to return home tearfully to Consett and in due course obtain lawful access to every penny of Edward's estate. Even that might not be necessary if things were in joint names or hers. There might, Annie speculated, be an odd will seeking to leave everything to the Prudhoe Pigeon Fanciers Association but there were no children and one would normally have expected everything to go Rosemary's way. Why on earth, then, should Rosemary go along with the notion that Edward's identity must be hidden and access gained to his fortune by securing transfers to a Belgian bank on the strength of a forged order? And this same logic would apply surely even if Rosemary and Arthur were in it together?

This last deduction was particularly upsetting for Annie for there was abundant evidence that they were in it together; at least, she corrected herself, in SOMETHING together. There was no getting away from the fact that they had planned meticulously to "elope" (was that a technical term, Annie asked herself, confined in its proper usage to unmarried striplings or could you still "elope" even though you were long wed and approaching retirement age?)

Annie slumped back in her chair and thumped her forehead with the heel of her hand. Just as things seemed to be coming together here was yet another conundrum. There was no escaping the fact that the events which had actually come about as a consequence of Edward's death were not the execution of any conspiracy concocted between Arthur and Rosemary. The original flight and the planning associated with it were certainly their joint endeavour – Arthur's secretary, Rosemary, had witnessed the signatures of himself and "his wife" on the transfers. But Annie was now forced to the conclusion that the events since Edward's death were the work of Arthur alone. Presumably it was opportunism on his part. He would realise, when Rosemary fell, perhaps in the course of a struggle, that the whole scene had changed and he would appreciate the new opportunities that had opened up. The corollary of that now struck Annie. In raiding Edward's funds by forged cheques and orders, Arthur was clearly running serious risks, perhaps for nothing unless he knew or at least believed that not only Edward but also Rosemary was dead and therefore unable to disrupt his plans. A Rosemary still alive would not take kindly to his abandonment of their original plan under which both benefitted and to his substitution therefore of his attempt to cheat Rosemary out of the Jenkinson inheritance. More important, she would easily be able to stop him. If, therefore, Arthur's stripping of Edward's body of all identification was part of the plan, albeit hastily concocted, for Arthur to gain access to Edward's funds for his, Arthur's, sole benefit he must have been sure, at that very time, that Rosemary would not be an obstacle to his plans. That meant that either he believed Rosemary to be already dead; or he was sufficiently within his powers to ensure that she soon would be.

Once bitten, twice shy. All this was conditioned upon the assumption, which was probable but not certain, that since Edward was the most likely victim he WAS the victim. Nevertheless it seemed to be a question of choosing between Edward wearing someone else's boot and someone else wearing Edward's stockings, trousers, Guernsey and anorak. Even mustering all due scepticism, Annie felt happy with her preference.

At that point in her rigorous review of what now appeared to be established, Dick came in.

"How's it going?" he asked.

Annie now felt she had known it all along. She was not at all surprised to hear herself reply:

"It's murder."

CHAPTER 18

It was, as will be readily understood; a bitter disappointment to Annie to be told that it was not murder or, more accurately, that Annie couldn't prove that it was.

She had no difficulty in persuading Dick that it was murder and even the Super now agreed that she should operate on an "all-systems-go" basis and get it all cleared up, top priority. By a well-known and much-used working criterion, the fact that it was murder and that Arthur had committed it was established, that is to say it was well past the point at which some policemen and even some Forces said "right, we've got our man; now let's prove it."

Annie recalled a celebrated case in Newcastle-upon-Tyne where a couple of thugs had been sent down for life and had moaned unceasingly about it ever since. Books, indeed, had been written, "proving" that they had been wrongly convicted and, indeed, they had. But the books had gone on to conclude that they were innocent and in that they were wrong. The police had got the right men alright (as they themselves subsequently admitted on release after serving their sentences) but they had assembled the wrong "proof" and although it satisfied the jury it offended against the accuseds' sense of justice.

Annie had "got her man" and she now had to prove it. To her, that meant not simply making out a case – any case that would persuade first, the Procurator Fiscal, then a jury. It meant finding out what had actually happened and how it had happened. And it meant putting the prosecution in a position of to satisfy the jury of both. As yet, she was not even in the position of having anything concrete to put before the Fiscal. He was no benign, shrewd, father figure in an ancient Harris Tweed suit. He was a pedantic and sometimes difficult Glasgow graduate, young for the job and aiming ultimately at higher things.

What was so irritating was that there was an eyewitness certainly to some of the crucial events and quite possibly to all. That was Rosemary. Sadly, there was no report off any further progress in restoring Rosemary's memory completely though, Alan had assured her, they were still working on it and far from abandoning hope; indeed, there seemed to be no reason why the amnesia should continue. These things often took a long time. The need for caution struck Annie. If all else failed then the case would ultimately depend upon such evidence as Rosemary was able to give. Rosemary might conceivably be in danger. She made a mental note to get in touch with the Glasgow force about that. They might think that at least "deterrent" protection might be in order.

Annie had every hope, however, that she would find an even better witness, Arthur himself. She had a fruitful line to follow. The Belgian bank must have a lead to Arthur. Even if he had covered his tracks pretty well, the money must be getting through to him, otherwise, why go to the trouble and risk. She was prepared, therefore, for the connection to be indirect and for there to be some burrowing to do. She was prepared, furthermore, for it to take some time for, although she hoped it would be a simple matter to get the relevant information from the Belgian bank, she was quite prepared to have to embark upon liaison with the Belgian authorities and even, perhaps, with Interpol. That invariably meant bureaucracy and confusion. If she could just pop over to Leuven herself and sort it out that would simplify things greatly, but the powers-that-be got very sensitive about trespassing on other peoples' jurisdictions.

She started, anyway, with a hopeful letter to the Belgian bank. She again committed the sin of courtesy. She thought it might lubricate the wheels if she wrote in a language that they would understand; besides that, as a matter of principle it embarrassed her the way we always addressed the continentals in English and expected them to reply in the same tongue. So she laboriously compiled the letter in her rusty academic French. In order to ensure that it was thoroughly comprehensible, she delayed until the following weekend before sending it in order that Tom could check it. His French was much better than hers. No it wasn't; he spoke excellent French and understood not a word of it as spoken by the ordinary French man or woman in the street. She, by contrast, found the language perfectly comprehensible but was too embarrassed ever to try to speak it. On the couple of occasions when they had been to the Western Alps together they had been like a double act.

Duly approved, the letter had gone off. A two-week delay had followed. Then a reply had arrived, couched in a language she had not, at first, recognised. She thought it was Dutch, wondered if it was German, then it finally dawned on her that it was Flemish, the "other" Belgian language. It had to go to Glasgow to be translated and although she telexed it to them, it had still taken several days for their version in English to come through. Annie had complained about this to Tom.

"I wouldn't mind so much if I hadn't gone to all that trouble to write it in French in the first place. You'd hardly expect them to reply in bloody Flemish, would you?"

"Oh, I could have told you that."

"How could you have told me that, smartarse?"

She could have kicked him when he said, "Well, you were writing to Leuven, weren't you."

"Louvain."

"Ah! Leuven, Louvain; it's not quite the same thing is it. One name Flemish, the other French, Walloon or what not. Point is, it's in Flanders, isn't it? If you'd written in English, they'd have replied in English; they all speak it fluently. The mistake you made was to write it in French. That would get their backs up. As a matter of principle, they would reply in Flemish – always do. I once nearly got to the Villa Lorraine in Brussels, only when my Flemish host rang to book a table – in Flemish, naturally - they persisted in using French and he put the phone down."

"Anyway" Annie changed the subject, "What am I supposed to do now?" for the reply, when translated, had done nothing more than announce the bank's policy not to disclose confidential details of their clients' accounts except in the circumstances prescribed by the relevant law, identified, as the Belgians still did it, unhelpfully by reference to number and date. With the "Dogs Act" or even the "Mr. Speaker George Thomas, Pension, Act" you knew where you stood, thought Annie. The Leuven letter did not even detail what the "prescribed circumstances by the relevant Law" were.

Should she now embark upon a lengthy correspondence, in English of course, asking what the "prescribed circumstances" were and then seeking to establish whether the circumstances of her case were among those prescribed, quite possibly with a lengthy and fruitless argument as to whether they were or not? Or should she seek the collaboration of Interpol or pass it over to the Belgian authorities to handle. Tom came to her rescue. "Look, let me see if I can do anything. I'm in Brussels next week. I could easily get out to Leuven for the little time it would take to get clear where you stand. It's only half an hour on the train. Who knows? They may even give me Arthur's address."

"It's Arthur."

"Come on. It has to be."

Not for the first time Annie wondered "Why Leuven?" It seemed an odd choice. A mediaeval university and the Stella Artois brewery was all she knew about it. The obvious choice would have been a well-established foreign banking centre and so far as she was aware, Leuven did not rank as that. Never mind, she had other things to attend to and for the next four days she set about working her way through the growing "in" pile of papers.

Tom rarely failed at anything. It was therefore an unusually bitter disappointment to receive his report on his return from Brussels.

"Very sorry, Annie. I tried; God knows I tried." Tom placed his hand melodramatically on his heart in a pathetic attempt to cheer her up and soften the blow a little. "But I could get sense neither into them nor out of them. I found out in Brussels before I went through to Leuven what the "prescribed circumstances" allowing them to disclose are. They include, as you would expect, some Belgian equivalent of 'information relating to the commission of an offence reasonably suspected of having been committed' and I thought 'Great; that should do the trick'. I expected to be in and out like a shot but I should have known better."

"First of all, they wanted to know who I was and what my authority was. I eventually got over that one, well, I think I did. I'm not sure. I told them I was "the advocate working in collaboration with and on behalf of the officer in charge of the Criminal Investigation Department of the Fort William Police Authority'. They seemed impressed enough by that but that's as far as I got."

"Isn't murder a 'serious offence' in Belgium then?" asked Annie.

"Well, it wasn't so much that. I explained what information 'we' needed and suggested that under the 'relevant law' it would be proper for them to provide information as (a) tending to establish the death or disappearance of the customer in question (that's apparently another of the 'prescribed circumstances' and (b) the 'serious crime' business. Our Jesuitical Belgian bank man then leapt on this and pointed out that his customer, whoever that might be, had manifestly not died or disappeared. Our 'Edward Jenkinson' might well have died or disappeared – that was none of his business. His, however, was alive and well and consuming transfers from his account from time to time, ergo he was sorry but he couldn't help us.

"What about the fact that your 'Edward Jenkinson' is reasonably suspected of having committed a serious crime' I asked him but he wanted to know what our proof was. I pointed out, correctly, though perhaps not very diplomatically, that we 'reasonably suspected' his man and that that was all that was required by HIS laws but he simply asked me what the basis of our 'reasonable suspicion' was and why, then, did we need to know the whereabouts of his man.

"I think that's where I made another mistake because I said:

'Well, because your man's evidence is essential to help us prove the case'.

'Ah,' he said, smugly 'my friend, we are locked in a circle. I am not allowed to help you, much as I might like.'

And when I asked him what he meant, he said 'You must have my man to have the serious crime and I must have the serious crime for you to have my man'.

"And the bugger just refused to be budged. I don't suppose it helped the cause much for me to mutter a few obscenities under my breath."

So there they were.

"I thought it was only the Swiss banks that played their cards as close to their chest as that," commented Annie.

"I rather think our little man in Leuven might have fancied himself as a budding gnome," was Tom's response to this. But the fact remained that they were, if not stuck fast, at least bogged down and having difficulty moving. There seemed nothing for it but Interpol or the Belgian fuzz. Still, Edward Jenkinson was good and dead and so far as they were aware Arthur Welsby would not be aware of their interest. There was no great hurry, Annie supposed, so it didn't matter all that much that it would take an aeon and two eras for them to do their stuff.

Then came Alan's news. They had made progress with

Rosemary. They now knew pretty well what had happened at the Gap that day. Annie was right to be on to Arthur.

"Look," Alan offered. "Any pretext to get up to the Ben for the day. I managed to get most of what she had to say on tape. Why don't I come up and set it all out for you? It's a bit complex to spell it all out over the 'phone?"

Annie had by this time taken a very distinct albeit platonic liking to Alan and would greatly have welcomed a visit from him even without the news that promised to explain everything. She readily agreed and Alan was on the road that same afternoon.

"You know, we're still going to need the help of your little man in Leuven," Annie reminded Tom. "Rosemary is unlikely to have kept tabs on Arthur's whereabouts during fifteen months of amnesia, is she?"

"No, but at least she should give us evidence that will make even the apprentice gnome move. Rosemary could hardly have timed it better from that point of view."

"No she couldn't," replied Annie adding, pensively, "It could hardly have been more convenient."

"How many famous Belgians are there?" asked Tom.

"Six," Annie told him. "Eddie Mercx, Hercule Poirot and three Breughels."

"Near enough," said Tom. "Let's get some lunch."

CHAPTER 19

"I'll tell you exactly how it happened," announced Alan to Annie and Tom. "At least as nearly as I can remember. Then you can have the *ipsissima verba* on the tape. Sorry we didn't get the whole thing on tape but I don't think it matters. Actually, Agnes Welsby had been to see her the day before and that might have given her a jolt.

As soon as he had realized that Rosemary had remembered more of what had happened on the Ridge that day, Alan had set up a tape machine. "Absolutely great," Annie exclaimed, delighted that for once in this whole messy business something had gone right. And for once, her expectations were not to be disappointed.

"Right then; Rosemary asked to see me," Alan began. The sister had told her I was in the hospital and would probably be calling in to see how she was getting on. Actually, I'd had little to do with the therapy. That was pretty well all Paul's doing (referring to his Glasgow colleague) but I timed my entrance well.

"I went along to see her and she said straight away 'Doctor, it's come back to me. I've got my memory back.' For a brief moment, she seemed chuffed then suddenly horrified and I thought she was going to go under again. She went on however. 'I can remember it all; everything that happened that day; on the Ridge that is. Oh God! It's terrible, it's unbelievable'. I tried to calm her down so the nurse could get the recorder there. Told her to relax, take it easy, take it step-by-step from the beginning. Not to press herself. Suggested a cup of tea. Asked her if she'd like a cigarette but she said she never smoked. She took it up at the point at which she and Arthur had reached the Gap. She knew what she had previously told us. Actually said 'I've told you about it all up as far as the Tower Gap, haven't I? I confirmed this. The nurse had arrived back with the tape-recorder - she'd been setting it up and by the time Rosemary was ready to go, so was she. I sent the nurse out for tea and then let Rosemary go. So this is it. There are a few lengthy silences but don't let that bother you. She takes it up again when she's ready."

Alan switched on the tape player and Annie heard Rosemary's voice for the first time. She was surprised at how deep and coarse it was.

"Well, we got to the Tower Gap and were having that stupid debate about who was going to lead it... I really couldn't understand Arthur. The men always do the leading. I've never led... I know the Gap is easy but psychologically it's the most testing part of the Ridge, isn't it? Sorry, do you know what I'm talking about?"

"Yes, yes. I do a bit of climbing," Alan's voice interrupted. "That's right. It is the most demanding part of the Ridge."

"I just thought it was peculiar, that's all..."

Alan, in Annie's office, interjected in a near whisper "I thought for a moment she was going to slip it here. Don't worry. She gets going again." She did:

"Then we heard this noise and looked up... " – another long pause followed by the sound of an intake of breath... "It was Edward... it was just as though we were watching a fantasy sequence in a film. He was standing there in his office suit and shoes with this new anorak on."

Alan, playing the surrogate detective: "Can you try to give me as much detail as you can. Don't worry about it. Don't press yourself. It doesn't matter if you can't."

"He was dressed like I say. Didn't have a hat or a helmet on. Had his suit trousers on. I assume his suit jacket as well. I couldn't see, of course... he was properly geared up though. I mean apart from the boots etc. He had his harness on and was tied on somewhere towards the last bit of the ridge."

Alan ("bless him" thought Annie) had then had the wit to ask, "Can you remember how he was tied on? It doesn't matter you know." (It did, in fact, matter a great deal) and Rosemary had continued:

"You know, like you do. He was tied on quite a way back. I don't remember how. Perhaps I couldn't see. But he just had a very long loop, a double rope, you know, looped through his harness and back to the belay... "

"What happened then?" Alan prompted. "Can you remember; did Edward say anything?"

"Oh, and he had his old sac on. The one he carries around in the back of the car... yes, he did. At first nobody said anything. It wasn't the sort of situation where you pass the time of day. Arthur said 'Edward?' sort of questioning. And Edward said – he looked furious – he said – he swore, actually I've never heard him swear like that before, use that word. Then he said 'you must be mad, you two. I can't believe that you could have possibly thought that you could get away with it' or something like that. Did we really expect, he asked... expect that he and Agnes would just sit there alone in Consett and do nothing about it. He went on, said a lot like that... we didn't know what to say. We still didn't understand what he was doing there… what he wanted. He still went on and on until he'd said it all. Neither of us had said anything at all. I think we were still stunned to see him there… we still didn't know why or even how he had known that we were there. Then I was beginning to get angry with him. I was just getting ready to tear a strip off him… beginning to hate him again.

"Then he continued. He started to talk a lot more reasonably. Said 'well this is no place to sort it all out. You'd better come on over. We'll go down. Agnes is in the car park. We've obviously got some sorting out to do. Come on over' and he flicked his rope back and stepped back a bit to make room for us… Arthur and I looked at one another. He sort of shrugged and set off to lower himself on to the block. Whatever ailment he had been suffering from seemed miraculously cured."

Suddenly the words came pouring out of Rosemary:

"It took him a bit of time to lower himself onto the block and drop his feet down to the foothold. He didn't hang about. Just leaned across straight away, got his hands onto the far wall then reached up and got the holds and started to pull himself up. Then it all happened at once. Just as he got his arm onto the top and started to pull himself up Edward suddenly stepped forward and took a kick at his head just like a footballer. Arthur managed to evade the full force of the kick but it struck him a glancing blow. Then, straight away – it all happened at once – Arthur grabbed Edward by the trouser leg – he may have been just trying to save himself – Edward was off balance from the kick. Arthur just tugged at him and he went straight over with a yell… then he was hanging there, on the rope, down the chimney."

There was then a long pause. They waited for about

thirty seconds before Alan gently nudged her.

"So there you were. You were at the low side of the Gap, tied on. Edward had gone over, down the Chimney. What did Arthur do? Where was he?"

"Oh… he was hanging on the far side. He groaned a bit… or swore… I think both. But he pulled himself up and slumped on the far side. He was half lying down, leaning, holding his head. We were like that for a long time. Then I heard Edward down the chimney. He can't have been all that far down. I heard him moan, just once, then he was quiet again. I yelled down at him. I called 'Edward, are you alright?' I didn't think he was very far down. I called down again but there was no response… I didn't say anything more… yes I did; I called out to Arthur. Eventually he got up still rubbing his head and groaning. I asked him 'Arthur, what are we going to do? What can we do? What about Edward?' Arthur didn't say anything. He kept rubbing his head. He looked at me, then down the chimney towards Edward. After a long time he looked across at me and said 'bloody Edward can look after himself' but I said 'no, we have to get him up. We'll sort it all out but we can't leave him there'. He wasn't far down; no more than fifteen to twenty feet I would say… Arthur still didn't say anything more for a long while. He kept looking at me and down the chimney. Then eventually he said something like 'ok, we'll get him up. I'll have to rope down to him. I can't get him up on the rope. I can't just heave up the dead weight.' This puzzled me a bit. Heaving him up on the rope seemed the obvious thing to do – there were two of us. But Arthur said 'I'll have to rope down and see if he's alright.'"

He said what he'd have to do was come back over to

my side and rope down off the block."

There now followed another long silence before Rosemary's voice resumed.

"So he did. He lowered himself down the holds. I think he climbed right down to the bottom of the Gap. Then he came up, onto and over the block and out onto my side again. He started to untie the rope and told me to do the same. He needed it to rope down, he said. He asked me if I was safe where I was sitting and I said I was. So he said 'right; untie yourself and let me have the rope. He took off the sac and put it down on the rock next to me, then took the rope and leaned over and took a belay running the double rope through it like you do. He nearly knocked the sac off so I put it on to be safe. Then he said 'right, here we go' and set off down. He was down there a long time. I kept asking if Edward was alright and he said 'yes', he was seeing to him. It was a long time. I asked him what he was doing and he shouted back impatiently that he was trying to see to Edward – he was unconscious. He sounded very angry. I shut up.

"The next thing I knew I heard something go thumping down the chimney. I yelled to Arthur and asked if he was alright. He yelled back 'yes, I'm alright but Edward's gone' I asked him what he meant and he said 'Edward's gone down the chimney. He fell; he came off. I was trying to get him up but he was unconscious. I couldn't hold him'. I wondered why if he'd slipped he hadn't just fallen back on the rope and ended up where he was before but I assumed Arthur had had to untie him or something. Or the rope had broken with the second fall. I don't know. I didn't know that is until Arthur came back up. 'What happened?' I asked him. 'He went down the chimney'

Arthur replied. I wanted to know how it had happened. Then Arthur said "cos it was the best place for him'. I asked him what he meant; but I knew what meant. I was just sitting there waiting while Arthur got the rope back. He tied himself into the belay and started to tie one end of the rope on. I reached out for the other end and Arthur said 'you needn't bother.' He was very cool and cold and I knew then that he was going to kill me. He'd killed Edward and he was going to kill me."

Alan went to the tape machine and played about with the 'fast forward' switch explaining that that was the last thing that Rosemary had said for several minutes. Eventually he found the place again and Rosemary's voice continued:

"All he said was 'I can't stand you Rosemary; never could.' Then he looked quickly up and down the ridge and grabbed at me. He tried to throw us off – he had tight hold of me and I couldn't get free. Once we'd gone, I kept hold of him... I must have screamed, I think. I remember us both going over but he was wrenched out of my hands when the rope took."

"He was tied on, of course, and had got her to untie."

"That's all," Rosemary concluded. "I can't remember falling. I can't remember it hurting. Funny, I thought I would."

Alan reached forward and stopped the tape. He pressed the rewind button. "Want to hear it again?" he asked.

"Later, not now." Annie put her hands to her cheeks. "So that's what happened?"

"That's what she says happened," corrected Tom.

"Yes, ok, but is there any reason to doubt her? She's just recovered her memory."

"No reason that I can think of," said Alan.

It was now clearly a murder investigation. Indeed, it

was almost a double murder investigation and Annie was now particularly careful to turn over every stone to make sure there was nothing nasty lurking underneath. Rosemary had eventually remembered it all. There was no reason whatever to suppose that what they had just listened to was a cock and bull story; but even if it was she would have had to remember in order to realise that a cock and bull story was needed. Nevertheless, she asked Alan:

"There can be no doubt, can there, that Rosemary Jenkinson was suffering from amnesia?"

"Well if she wasn't, she must be an incredible actress and I'm sure that's not the case."

Extremely cautious by reason of her experience with the case thus far Annie asked, "So we can believe what she said?"

Alan thought long and hard then stated his opinion. "You can believe it alright. I was there when she told it. I had a close eye on her every second."

"Except when you were fiddling with the machine," corrected Annie.

"Ok, almost every second," continued Alan with a sigh. "She was and still is a sick woman. She appears to know nothing about the circumstances of this business except such facts as are within her personal knowledge and she can remember. She is either an extraordinarily talented dissembler with phenomenal patience or she is absolutely genuine. After all, as you say, why would she lie?"

CHAPTER 20

The three of them, Annie, Tom and Alan had dinner together that evening. They tried to talk about other things and largely succeeded. It was however inevitable that they should return from time to time to the day's earlier events.

"She was wearing the sac?" Tom offered, "When he threw her over, I mean."

"You mean he probably unwittingly threw away all his ill-gotten gains?" queried Annie.

"No, I wasn't so much thinking that though now you mention it, I suppose it's likely. Where do you keep your valuables on the hill, Alan?"

"Lid of the sac."

"Me too," added Annie. "Learned the hard way. Lost too much out of pockets."

"Yes, well," mused Tom "That makes it all the more likely. No, I was thinking that the sac would probably identify Arthur. Anyway Arthur would rather Rosemary wasn't found, or at least identified, wouldn't he? What I'm getting at is that it was a rather opportunistic killing on Arthur's part wasn't it? I don't mean to say that he hadn't had it in mind. I reckon now he had. The strange business of him asking her to lead across the Gap, you know. But the way it came about, he would realise immediately, wouldn't he, that he had some tidying up to do" And if his valuables were in the sac, he'd have to go and find it, wouldn't he?"

They agreed and then were distracted by the scallops mornay. It was several minutes before Alan returned to the topic.

"Do you think Arthur ever intended to shack up with Rosemary? I'm thinking about what he said to her on the Ridge; just before he threw her off. Didn't he say he couldn't stand her – had always hated her, something like that?"

Tom threw it back at him. "Dunno. What do you think; you're the shrink?"

"It does help actually to have met your patient, you know," Alan retorted, a reflex defence immediately lowered, "but from what we know of him, I wouldn't be at all surprised if he was appalled at the change which Rosemary was proposing to bring about in his life. Come to think of it, I'd be astonished if he weren't. He really does seem to be a very staid, stick-in-the-mud sort, doesn't he? He'd want the absolute minimum of disruption in his life."

"Why on earth would he agree to it then?" Annie asked. "Seems very odd to me. He can hardly have been a stick-in-the-mud on this one. All he had to do was to say "no" to Rosemary wasn't it? Anyway, hadn't he taken a great liking to his nooky?"

"That's not at all incongruous," Alan had insisted. "He's a weak man, isn't he? That's what comes through more strongly than anything. Everything we know about him points in that direction. Hasn't he just gone along with every breeze, even the lightest ones, which has blown on his life? His marriage, his career. The stark ordinariness of his life; Rotary, Masons, all that. A woman like Rosemary – determined, knowing what she wanted etc. – would find him easy to manipulate. So far as we can see, she did do all the manipulating, didn't she? If it hadn't been for the clothes they wore. You'd have thought she was the man of the pair."

"You're still ignoring the nooky," Annie reminded him.

"Sorry but no. I don't think that makes any difference. Sure, he liked his nooky. Not surprising, is it? He had a lot of lost time to make up for. But that's no reason whatever for supposing that he would want to shack up with Rosemary. He probably only got it up because he wasn't shacked up with her, because she was forbidden fruit. An awful lot of men, at least men of Arthur's age, are like that. They think of having it off as naughty and a 'bit' has to be 'on the side' for it to appeal. If it's not 'on the side' it's not naughty and if it's not naughty there's no appeal. What Arthur said to Rosemary, the last thing he said to her, was probably absolute Gospel. He probably did detest her every minute of the day when they weren't actually on the job. Ask yourselves is there any evidence whatever that's Rosemary had any appeal whatever for Arthur beyond the one thing?"

"I can't believe that the man you're describing could do what Arthur did on the Ridge, that's my problem," Tom contributed. "That wasn't weak, was it?"

"Oddly, it was," explained Alan. "At least, it was the act of a weak man, a weak man who allowed himself to be backed into an impossible position. A man with more guts, more character, would never find himself in such a position. I'm not saying the ACTS were weak. I'm saying simply that they were desperate and the weak man can despair just like anyone else; probably more so than anyone else." Lightening the tone, he joked "I'm not a weak man; I refuse to be backed into a corner over this. I want a coffee and a large Armagnac."

They sat and drank and smoked, tacitly not to allowing murder to intrude upon their mellowness. It was only shortly before they were more or less ready to go that Tom raised it again:

"I suppose it's back to the Belgian bank man again now," addressing it to Annie.

"Well it's clearly Arthur we want, isn't it? Leuven's the only lead we've got. Fancy another trip?"

"I rather think you'd be better advised to appoint another envoy next time," he counselled. "I'm afraid I may have queered your pitch there. I'm sure the gnome of Leuven would be better approached by someone other than yours truly."

"There's a problem about your going, is there Annie?" asked Alan.

"'Fraid so," replied Annie, "protocol and all that. How about you?"

It was not a serious request and, anyway, it was not up Alan's street.

"An Interpol job, then, or something like that, is it?" Tom asked.

"I suppose so," said Annie, but it did not carry conviction.

CHAPTER 21

"Prospect Cottage, Healaugh, Nr. Reeth, North Yorkshire," yelled Annie.

"What's that?" asked Dick.

"His address. Mr. Edward Jenkinson's current address. Hang on while I go and see the Super."

"My God; that was quick. How did you manage that?" Dick asked, quite overwhelmed by the unaccustomed efficiency of these foreign police johnnies.

"Oh, intelligent, efficient detective work," Annie had claimed.

"Oh, come on," Dick complained. "How did you manage it?"

"I just wrote them; simple."

"Wonders never cease! You just wrote them and politely asked for his address and they gave it to you?"

"I didn't say that."

"Oh, come on; stop being mysterious. How'd you get it?" asked Dick.

Smug, if a little guilty, Annie swore him to secrecy and told him.

Arriving at the office the day following Alan's visit with Rosemary's tape, Annie was fighting off second thoughts about the idea that had seemed so attractive when viewed through a glowing alcoholic mist. Caution and propriety were striving to reassume control. Momentarily they won and she set about the laborious business of taking advice as to whether to work through the Belgian authorities or Interpol. After almost an hour searching fruitlessly for the number or address to which to refer, the original idea counter-attacked and won and she turned to her typewriter.

The letter that she wrote to the Leuven bank bore Tom's Edinburgh address and it was signed by "Annie Chisholm, secretary". It announced that for the next six months and perhaps indefinitely, Edward Jenkinson would be residing at and carrying on business from the above address. It asked the bank to note the change of address, to address all future communications to the new address. And it asked them to confirm receipt of the instruction and its effect.

Annie had grave doubts about the propriety of this. About all that was free from doubt was her judgment that if she had sought authority to write it, it would have been refused. There was a stench of impropriety about it but Annie could see nothing illegal in it. She had used an actual address, albeit Tom McIntyre's and not "Edward Jenkinson's" and Annie Chisholm certainly existed if not employed by "Edward Jenkinson", at least not employed in the way the letter implied. And so far as she was aware it was not an offence in Scots law to screw out of a tight-lipped Belgian bank information which that bank was obliged by Belgian law to provide. Even so, her reservations were such that she had not sought Tom's permission until the letter was posted. It was as well; his Edinburgh advocate's caution more than curbed his enthusiasm for the idea. At least, bless him, he knew a *fait accompli* when he saw one and had undertaken to send through any news as soon as he got it. He gave it as his candid opinion that it was extremely unlikely that any news would be forthcoming. But his experience was of the bossman, who had probably got where he was largely by keeping his mouth shut. Annie had banked on her request being treated as a minor administrative matter to be handled in normal course without need to refer it upwards. And it had worked.

Taking Tom's earlier advice she had written in English. It had not worked (that was another one she had put over on him). They had replied in Flemish, as before, only this time she had not needed a translation. She could read what mattered because it was in English – Tom's Edinburgh address and, magic!

"Prospect Cottage,
Healaugh,
Nr. Reeth,
North Yorkshire,
United Kingdom."

The rest she could infer. It took only a couple of hours for the police in Richmond to check that the occupant was in residence and ring back and tell her.

For once, the Super was co-operative:

"Right; what are you waiting for? Off you go."

"Oughtn't we to liaise with Richmond?" Annie had asked, anxious not to cock it up right at the end.

"Don't bother about that," he had insisted. "I'll set it up with them. There'll be no problem there." (Annie wondered if her Consett experience was typical of northern England). "It's a straightforward business isn't it? We know all about it and they know nowt."

Annie confirmed that this was the case.

"Right, then, they'll want somebody there but that's all. Give me an ETA and I'll arrange for you to be met."

Annie made a quick calculation. She decided she might as well take the A66 across to Scotch Corner. It made sense to head straight for the police station in Richmond and pick up an escort there. They would appreciate her concern for their convenience.

"And Annie,"

"Yes Super?"

"Take it steady. Don't go barging in. He's killed once and nearly twice already. Remember, until he says 'It's a fair cop; I done it' you don't know anything for sure."

She appreciated that. She said "thanks" and within half an hour she and Dick were heading south in one of the new Sierras.

They were waiting for her in Richmond and a front-row forward vying for a place ion the county side was assigned to accompany them. Except for a quick stop to pick up a couple of abominable motorway hamburgers and two cans of fizz, they had driven straight through.

The front-row forward was curious to know if a scrum was likely. "What sort of bloke is he then Miss, do you know?"

"Oh, we don't expect any trouble, if that's what you mean," Annie reassured him. "Retired bank manager, pushing sixty."

Not quite what the front-row forward had expected. "And he's done a couple of blokes in, pushing 'em off a mountain?"

"Well, a man and a woman. And he failed with the woman but, yes, that's the gist of it."

"The front-row forward took the whole of the drive up the dale to digest this and wonder what, if any, its significance was for him.

Within fifteen minutes they were in Reeth. As they drove up the short hill, through the green, Annie felt a twinge of regret that it had taken such a sordid business such as that to get her back to Swaledale. It was the starkest and at times the dourest of the Dales and you probably had to have peculiar tastes to appreciate it but it suited her alright. She remembered sing-songs in the Black Bull on Saturday nights accompanied by Betty at the piano playing with the universal left-hand; the same repetitious bass chord no matter what the melody. Then they were through the village, past the school and in no time dropping down to Healaugh.

It was the front-row forward who had earlier driven in to check for signs of habitation and he was able to direct them straight to Prospect Cottage. "Edward Jenkinson" had chosen a good place for a hideaway. Not many knew of Healaugh's existence, not even, remembered Annie, William the Conqueror whose Domesday Book had stopped short at the forest which started between Reeth and Healaugh. And even those who did would not be in the least surprised to find a retired, elderly bank manager taking up residence there. Few of the cottages were permanently occupied these days. In the majority of those that were lived exactly such people as "Edward", folk retired from the grim conurbations of Yorkshire and the north-east determined to spend as much time in the Dale as possible in the few years remaining to them.

It was a gloomy day and the light was on in the downstairs room as Dick opened the gate for the three of them to walk the few steps up a stone-flagged path to the front door. Annie took a deep breath and knocked.

CHAPTER 22

The door opened and there, at last, stood the man they were after. The description had made no reference to a beard. That would have been added as a first cautious step in disguise registered Annie. He was, she thought pedantically, "balding" rather than "bald" and he was scruffier than she had expected, though she immediately realized that her expectation of seeing a white-collar worker as though fresh from the bank was misplaced. He looked from Annie to Dick, to the uniformed front-row forward then back to Annie and asked simply:

"Yes?"

"Mr. Edward Jenkinson?" Annie enquired cautiously.

"Yes, that's me," he asserted.

"I'd better introduce us. My name is Chisholm, Inspector Chisholm and, turning to Dick, "this is Sergeant Todd. We're from Scotland and" Annie realized with embarrassment that she had forgotten his name. He came to her rescue. "Helliwell, Constable Helliwell, Richmond."

"Sergeant Todd and I are from Fort William, Mr. Jenkinson."

He was not surprised. He said nothing. He did not invite them in. He did not ask their business. The change in the tone of his skin told them he knew.

"May we come in?"

He pushed open the door behind him and went in leaving it to them to follow. They did so.

He turned to face them. Annie started. "Mr. Jenkinson, we are investigating a serious crime committed on Ben Nevis in October 1983 and..." she decided to stick to the hallowed, safe phrase... "we have reason to believe that you may be able to help us with our inquiries."

Before she had finished, he had eased himself onto one of the chairs surrounding the scrubbed pine kitchen table and leaned forward, burying his head in his hands. They heard a muffled "Oh, God!" There was no struggle, verbal or otherwise. It was over.

"You're not Edward Jenkinson, are you?" she now asked.

At first he did not move. Then, raising his head only slightly and looking not at them but at the stone fireplace in front of him he started:

"You know I'm not, don't you?" There was a long pause whilst they left it to him to continue.

"I'm glad you've come at last. I've been wanting to get it all settled. I didn't kill him, you know, at least not intentionally. He just suddenly had a go at me like a lunatic. All I did was to defend myself. I know, I must have gone a bit mad but you don't stop and think in a crazy situation like that. Can you imagine? His first attack knocked me flat. I got up; I hadn't a clue what was happening but I had the wit to grab a piece of scree, must have been the size of an orange, and I just swung it at his head. It was a direct hit and he collapsed. When I looked, there was a hole where his temple used to be and his eyeball was hanging out on his cheek. I didn't see it happening. I only knew what I'd done after I'd done it. Then I panicked. I had to make sure he'd never be found. I didn't think that anybody would find him. It's been fifteen months; I was sure it was over. I still can't believe that you found him. I dragged him up tight under a low wall topped by scree. I must have pulled several tons down on top of him".

They were puzzled by this account He must have somehow have dragged him up beneath the screes on the summit tower and buried him there. But the scree was constantly on the move and the body must have made its way down into the chimney, in the thaw, probably.

"Exactly where did you bury him, Mr. Welsby?"

Momentarily perplexed, he answered, "Where you found him. At the bottom of Tower Gully... What did you call me?"

Annie, now thoroughly puzzled, told him "Welsby. You're Arthur Welsby aren't you?"

He paused, then grasped at what registered as a half-chance to escape justice at the eleventh hour. "No, no, my name's not Welsby. You've got the wrong man. My name's Gerrard, Ken Gerrard. Look, I can prove it."

It was very slow going at first. Gerrard realized they were in the dark and clung onto his hope of a last-minute reprieve stubbornly. Gradually, shuffling the evidence around and alternatively coaxing and hinting at the dire consequences of failure to co-operate they pieced it together.

Gerrard had finally steeled himself to make the move across the Gap and, inexplicably elated at the feat for one who just a few hours previously had been contemplating a solo ascent of Point Five Gully, headed off for the summit. He had decided to go down via Tower Gully and was descending from the summit following the edge of the escarpment looking for the start when his gaze was distracted by a something falling from the direction of Tower Ridge below and to his left. It went looping down at first, then seemed almost to stop as it slithered on scree before continuing its fall down Tower Gully. He had to overcome his incredulity finally to recognize that It was a body. It was, of course, Rosemary.

The body kept going and going, dwindling beneath his gaze until finally it slithered and juddered down scree for another fifty yards or so before coming to a halt almost exactly opposite the terrace that leads to the start of the gully below the Douglas Gap. And there it stayed without moving.

"Jesus Christ," thought Gerrard. "What the hell am I going to do?" He knew, however, what he had to do. The sight of Rosemary's progress down the gully in front of him chastened him and he picked his way cautiously down scree that normally would hardly have hindered his progress. It took him over an hour. Eventually he neared to body. It had still not moved. It was not to be expected after a fall like that, that it would. As he approached it, he saw help coming from below. A figure strode from the direction of the Ridge towards him. Gerrard bent down over the broken body. It looked like a woman. A cursory glance seemed to confirm his fears for her life and he called out to the nearing figure "She's had it, I'm afraid" and set about trying to find some identification from the sac.

The next thing he knew was that something knocked him off his feet and he was sliding down the Gully, a stinging pain in his shoulder. An involuntary somersault thrust him onto his feet just as the figure charged at him again and he realized, to his utter amazement that he was being attacked. His initial account of what followed next was true. By the time his terrified frenzy had subsided, Arthur Welsby was well and truly dead.

For God knows how long Gerrard was in a crisis of indecision. He had done nothing wrong, had he? The sensible thing was clearly to go down, report exactly what had happened and lead the police back up to the scene of the slaughter but the terror of authority which had dogged his whole life made him hesitate. Authority's judgment on him had always assumed the worst. What would they make of it if he went in and reported that a woman had just happened to fall in front of him and get herself killed and whilst he was seeing what, if anything, he could do to help, this bloke had attacked him and he had killed him?

Nevertheless, he told himself, that was what he had to do. When he first started to go through her sac he had only the vaguest notions about identifying them so as to be able to tell the police who they were. In the inside pocket of Welsby's anorak he found a wallet containing cash, credit cards and a cheque book, the stubs of which recorded a credit balance of proportions unknown to Gerrard, a driving license, car key and other items indicating that the man he had killed was Edward Jenkinson.

In the lid of Rosemary's sac he found, amongst other things, a thick, stiff, buff envelope. Opening it, he discovered more than £40,000 in large denomination notes and two bankers' drafts, payable to bearer, totalling more than £90,000. The rest of the contents consisted of anonymous mountain gear except for an odd black shoe. He was a rich man; all idea of doing the right thing and involving the police disappeared but he had to cover his tracks.

He immediately conceived what he thought at first was a brilliant idea. Tie the two bodies together so as to make it look as if both had fallen but immediately realized that, so far as he knew, they were strangers. As well, he imagined the two bodies on slabs in the morgue, one blackened with bruises and broken-boned, the other unmarked except for a hole where the temple should have been and an eyeball resting on a cheek.

He then turned to search all the gullies and crags for signs of any other climbers but could detect not another soul anywhere. He then looked around nearer to where he stood and found a low crag that was nothing more than an interruption in a continuous scree slope. First looking around again to make sure that all was clear, he dragged "Jenkinson's" body across the scree towards the low wall. He spent some minutes hollowing a crude grave beneath the wall, dragged the body into it and threw in a few rocks after it.

Then he climbed cautiously above the wall and set about pulling down the keystones which were holding up the scree above. Several times he succeeded in dislodging great loads of scree so that it poured over the wall, covering the body.

Only when he had reduced the wall to half its former height did he stop. When he later guided Annie there, they found Arthur Welsby's body exactly as described by Gerrard. Stuffing all the items, which could have identified the bodies into his sac he then headed off down the Allt a'Mhuillin. Although it was getting dark he had no difficulty in finding, in the golf club car park the car to which the key found in Jenkinson's wallet belonged. He threw his sac in the back and, seeing himself under observation by two golfers at a nearby vehicle quickly got in and drove off.

He had no plan more specific than just getting away. He headed south stopping only for petrol until the irresistible need for sleep compelled him to park in a lay-by. Only when he awoke the following morning, his mind refreshed, did he turn to the question of where he was getting away to. He realized that he was a rich man and could go anywhere. He drove on heading for Dover but then realized, as he approached the Dartford Tunnel that the car might link him to "Jenkinson". He therefore headed into London intending to park it in a quiet side street. He did so and headed, with his sac, to the nearest Tube station. The car has never been found.

From London, Gerrard made his way by train to Dover. He boarded the first ferry leaving Dover which took him to Ostend. There, feeling safer at last, he pondered briefly what he might do next. Train signs in the Ostend station reminded him of Leuven where he had once spent a month on an exchange visit and the student life of which had appealed to him.

He stayed in Leuven only long enough to establish that the account he had opened in Jenkinson's name had received, in addition to the sterling notes credited to it the proceeds of the two drafts. He then headed off, first to the Alps and from there to the Himalayas where he had come within an ace of being recognized by one of his former Nottingham club-mates. Soon bored with the Himalayas, he eventually decided that he could safely return to the United Kingdom. After considering the relative obscurity of Mid-Wales, Galloway and the Dales he settled upon the latter where his past finally caught up with him in the form of a pretty, petite Scottish policewoman.

CHAPTER 23

It may be of interest to know what subsequently happened to some of the characters with which this account has been concerned most of whom survived the events with which it deals.

Not, sadly, Greg Douglas whose body was found on Creagh Meaghaich shortly after those events. A carved stone commemorating his short life and recording his death was placed on the mountain by his parents.

Sandy Piper is alive and well and still knocking off Munroes although much less regularly than of old. He married the "dark lady" over the border and now helps her run their antique shop in Alnwick.

Ken Gerrard will shortly be released from prison. It was eventually decided (rightly, of course) not to prosecute him for murder, perhaps cynically on the grounds that he was the only witness and a prosecution would likely fail. He was, however, successfully prosecuted for the theft of the Jenkinson and Welsby fortunes. To me, the sentence looks harsh. The money was recovered practically intact. After an initial fling Gerrard was learning, late in life, to exercise a little self-discipline and make it last. Apart from the cottage, which actually increased in value, he spent little more than the interest on the capital. The balance was duly returned *in toto*. I have always thought that a part of the sentence imposed on him was in respect of that part of his involvement in the affair to which no criminal liability attached.

Alan is back at work. Tom proposed to Annie. She rejected him still offering as her reason that she knew him too well and still not sure what she meant. They nevertheless bought a cottage just beyond Glencoe and live together every weekend and holidays. Alan and I see them often and they occasionally condescend to climb with us. I still lust after Annie. At least, I think I do but it may just be a trace of memory.

Annie dropped the idea of prosecuting Andrew McNee. He owes that to Tom. Tom argued that unless Annie could prove beyond a reasonable doubt that McNee intended not to return to the Fairmont when he left that morning, he could not be convicted. Tom also thought that McNee's case was ripe to establish the existence of the crime of attempted manslaughter but Annie considered that too academic to waste her valuable time on.

McNee went back to Preston to resume his business with an almost clear conscience and has gone from strength to strength.

Agnes and Rosemary spend their winters in a modest villa near Soller in Majorca though the modesty is not necessary for they are quite well off. As is stated above, Agnes recovered most of the money from the Leuven account plus, of course, the proceeds of sale of the cottage in Healaugh and the house in Consett. Whoever bought out Arthur's pension must be kicking himself. Rosemary also did quite well. The house, plus Edward's share of the firm, plus the proceeds of sale of a few investment properties left her comfortably off. Every spring, they transfer to their rose-bestrewn stone gatehouse lodge on the shores off Loch Leven. It is small, only two bedrooms, but it is more than adequate for them. The other bedroom, the guest room, is rarely needed.

Most spring and summer evenings, they sit there, one

on each side of the log-fire. Tom, Annie and Alan agree that it is odd, although understandable, that two lonely, ageing widows should have put differences behind them and decided to spend the rest of their lives together. After all, they had no other friends and, in their previous existences, with their less than fulfilling husbands, life was not exactly ecstatic.

I do not think it is at all odd, although I do agree that they complement each other. Agnes cooks and looks after the house; Rosemary is usually either gardening or tinkering with her vintage motorcycle in the garage. We often pass that way and I have seen her nostalgically pruning her roses with her trusty old Swiss army knife, which has seen a variety of uses in its time. They seem more settled and contented than they ever were before in their more conventional unions. I imagine them sitting there of an evening nursing a cognac and a beer smiling at one another. I hear a sigh and an occasional giggle of relief as they recall how, in the autumn of 1983 Rosemary found herself confronted by an unexpected situation. Her husband was at her mercy unconscious down Glover's Chimney and Arthur was still reeling, holding his head suffering the consequences of Edward's flying kick to the head. Had she observed the precept of protecting oneself even against the unforeseen perhaps Ken Gerrard's unwitting intervention would not have been necessary to ensure a happy life together for Agnes and Rosemary, freed from the shackles off marriage to two dull, inept and unfortunate men who met with death on Ben Nevis.

Published by

www.publishandprint.co.uk